1,000
Reasons
NEVER
to Kiss
a Boy

1,000 Reasons NEVER to Kiss a Boy

MARTHA FREEMAN

HOLIDAY HOUSE / NEW YORK

Library of Congress Cataloging-in-Publication Data
Freeman, Martha, 1956–
1,000 reasons never to kiss a boy / by Martha Freeman.—1st ed.
p. cm.
Summary: After her first boyfriend cheats on her,
sixteen-year-old Jane vows to never kiss another boy.
ISBN-13: 978-0-8234-2044-5 (hardcover)
[1. Dating (Social customs)—Fiction.   2. Interpersonal relations—
Fiction.   3. Friendship—Fiction.]   I. Title.   II. Title: One thousand
reasons never to kiss a boy.
PZ7.F87496Aah 2007
[Fic]—dc22
2006019538

For Mary Cash,
who never lost faith
in "the bagel book"

Chapter One

Reason One: Because a boy will betray you in a walk-in fridge when all you wanted was sliced tomatoes, and when this happens, you will be too surprised and mad and confused to move, let alone give him the quick kick in the garbanzos he so totally deserves.

You're probably wondering how come a heterosexual girl with normal hormone levels—me, I mean—would decide to list reasons never to kiss a boy.

It started yesterday, which, not coincidentally, is the identical day I caught my boyfriend, Elliot, in the walk-in fridge kissing Valerie, who—as everybody who works with us at Seymour's Bagels knows from personal observation—has a tattoo of a red butterfly between the dimples on her butt.

Elliot and I had had a fight in the morning. It was after the lunch rush that I went to the fridge for tomatoes and found him there in a clinch with the tattoo queen.

I exited the fridge. I started to cry. My friend Arthur untied the bandanna he wears for work and gave it over so I could wipe the tears off my face. The bandanna smelled good, like herbal conditioner. When I returned it, Arthur shook it out and gave it back and said I should keep it because I would need it again.

Then he said, "You know, Jane, there will always be girls like Valerie. The trick is not to fall for a guy like Elliot."

1

And I said, "Thanks a lot. How come you didn't tell me that like four months ago—when Elliot and I started going out?"

Arthur sighed. "You wouldn't have listened," he said. "People in love never do."

And he was right.

Elliot Badgi was my very first boyfriend. Till he came along, I was famous for being the girl who didn't care so much about boys. I mean, I watched my friends hooking up and getting sappy, breaking up and melting down—and I said to myself: Who needs the aggravation? I'd rather hang out with Stacy and Amy or read a book or download the latest from Bomb-Sniffing Dogs. I'd rather study, even.

Then Elliot shined his gorgeous eyes on me, and something inside lit up like the sun had touched it, and I said to myself, Wow—this must be why people put up with the worry and the suffering and the drama.

Arthur was right. I used to be Jane-in-love.

Now I was Jane-in-despair.

I wasn't much good at work after that. Shuja let me go home early. When I got there, John and Mitch were on the job, same as they were when I left in the morning. John and Mitch are two of the crew from Very-Nice Construction, the crew that has been remodeling my mom's and my house since a few seconds after the big bang. I know all their names by now, and the names of their wives and kids. I see more of John—he's the foreman—than I do of Mom.

"Hey, Janey, why the long face?" John looked down at me from a ladder. He was restapling the plastic sheet that separates

2

the dining room and kitchen—construction zone—from the rest of the house.

"No reason," I said. "I'm fine."

John looked back at the ceiling. "That boyfriend o' yours?" he asked.

"How did you know?"

John tugged at the plastic to make sure it was secure, then he climbed down. He smiled—a big smile on a small face. He is a couple of inches shorter than me and wiry. He tapped his paint-spattered ball cap with his finger. "Power of deduction," he said. "If it was the school year—smart, ambitious girl like you—I'd think you were upset about your calculus grade. But it's summertime. Seymour's not gonna be firing his star employee, so what's left? Gotta be boyfriend trouble." John knelt by his toolbox to put away the staple gun. "Wanna talk about it?"

From beyond the plastic wall, Mitch hollered at him. "Whadda we do about this countertop? Trash or garage?"

"It's okay," I told John. "I'll be fine."

"Trash!" John yelled at Mitch. Then he looked up at me. "Course you will, Janey. One thing about boyfriend trouble, it's seldom fatal."

I didn't smile, but I made a noise that was supposed to be a laugh. "Right now I kind of wish it was."

John straightened up and looked into my face. "I know," he said. His eyes were so sympathetic, I thought he might even give me a hug. It would have been okay, too. According to my mom, John is the world's greatest dad. He has four little kids and coaches every sport they play. He even changes diapers.

3

I thought of my own dad. He and my mom are divorced. He hasn't lived with us since I was little. I don't mean this is some big tragic abandoned-kid story, though. My dad only lives twenty miles away, and I see him all the time on weekends. If I called and said, "Help!" he'd come running.

Still. It's not the same as having him here.

The moment passed. John didn't hug me. Instead, he clapped me on the shoulder like I was one of his little soccer stars. "I guess it's no use an old fart telling you you'll get over him?" he said. "He wasn't good enough for you, anyway. Honest truth, I didn't like him so well."

"You didn't? But he was . . . he was . . . ." Now the tears cut loose again, and I reached for Arthur's bandanna. "He was *perfect!*"

"Aw, Janey. You poor kid. Nobody's perfect, honey. . . ." John said more stuff that was supposed to be comforting, but I wasn't listening. I was hiding my face behind the bandanna and picturing Elliot—the way he leans back and holds his ribs when he's laughing, the way his expression turns soft when he looks at me after a kiss, the way his eyebrows form a V when he's thinking.

"He's so different from other guys," I told John between sobs. "More . . . I don't know . . . mature maybe? More interesting? The way he's brave about stuff that scares me, the way he made these little romantic gestures like asking me out for dessert instead of burgers . . . how everybody else plays baseball or soccer, and he *fences.* He can dance, and he even *smelled good. . . .*"

"Let me get you a glass of water," John said.

In our house these days, getting a glass of water is not so easy. What's left of our kitchen is beyond the plastic wall, what my mom and I call no-woman's-land. So for the past month, our refrigerator has lived in a corner of the living room, and the cans and boxes and dishes that should be in the kitchen cupboards are on bookshelves. We don't have a stove. When we cook, we cook in the microwave, which is on a card table along with paper plates and plastic forks.

John went to the bookcase for a glass and to the refrigerator for ice. Then he had to go into the downstairs bathroom for water out of the sink.

"Better?" he asked after I took a long drink.

"Not so thirsty, anyway."

"Do you want anything else? A bowl of Lucky Charms?" he asked.

That made me smile. John's been around so much, he knows practically everything about me—like how I'd eat cereal for breakfast, lunch, and dinner if Mom let me. "No, thanks," I said. "I think I'll just go upstairs and see what's new with the band."

The sound of Mitch's sledgehammer rang in my ears as I climbed the stairs to my room. Very-Nice Construction had already finished in there—put in hardwood floors and painted, replaced the windows. I have to say it looks a lot nicer than it used to with stained shag carpeting and ugly wallpaper. Mom even got me a new computer desk to replace the yard-sale table I used to have.

I fired up my computer, and in a few seconds I was scanning the website of my favorite band, Bomb-Sniffing Dogs. Since I had last checked, there were a dozen new postings. I skimmed them. A couple were from newbies, and most were from the loser regulars who don't have lives beyond the boxes that hold their sound systems.

Of course, I thought, maybe that last thought was just the tiniest bit mean?

I mean, with Elliot gone, did *I* have a life?

Let us take inventory.

It was 4:17 P.M. on Wednesday, July 26, exactly one month before the annual Kickoff Parade that marks the beginning of football season here in College Springs, Pennsylvania. I, Jane Greene, was sixteen years, four months, and twenty-seven days old. My first boyfriend, Elliot, had dumped me for a girl who applies her eye makeup with Magic Marker.

What did I have left?

1. Best girlfriends Stacy and Amy
2. Best not-girlfriend Arthur
3. Job at Seymour's Bagels
4. $812.43 in my bank account
5. More or less permanent place on the high school honor roll
6. Mom, Dad, Grandma, Bruce

I don't know, World, what do you think?
Does that add up to a life?

Overnight I had this dream. And in this dream there was an epiphany, which is a word that has about a 20 percent probability of showing up on the SAT and means "a sudden vision of life-altering truth." In my case it was a pink neon billboard rising like a mirage from the desert, and it was all glowing and read 1,000 REASONS NEVER TO KISS A BOY.

It was—get it?—a sign.

But it's lunchtime today before I figure out what I'm supposed to do about it. I am back at Seymour's working the sandwich counter, making a ham and Gruyère with honey mustard on ciabatta, when it comes to me.

I am supposed to compile a list, a thousand reasons never to kiss a boy.

I think back to the Sunday school lesson about Moses. When God said ten commandments, did he maybe wish God had said five? Because I am definitely thinking one thousand is *a lot* of reasons.

But a sign is a sign. You don't argue with these things. Till now, I didn't know what I was supposed to do with my life. But here—at last—is my meaning and purpose. A thousand reasons never to kiss a boy. It will be my life's work.

Chapter Two

Reason Two: Because when he dumps you, which he will because dumping girls is the nature of boys, it will make you remember all the sad, pathetic things that made you a reject in the first place.

This is the complete story of my love life, which will not take long because even though I am sixteen years old, until Elliot came along, I had never been kissed. On the lips, I mean. Except by relatives. And usually then only if they were aiming at my cheek and missed.

I don't want you to think, though, that no boy ever showed any romantic interest in me before that. One did. His name was Josh Silberman.

It was first grade. It was the cafeteria. It was lunchtime. Josh Silberman was sitting next to me, and he pulled a Star of David necklace out of his pocket and said, "Here. It means we're getting married."

I remember my mom had packed me an egg salad sandwich that day. I was chewing. It is amazing to me now that a boy could get romantic with a girl chewing egg salad.

I don't think I had been thinking about marriage at that moment. Probably I had been thinking more about a new outfit for my Flight Attendant Barbie and whether I would ever get the hang of Miss Mary Mack all dressed in black. But Josh Silberman wasn't that gross for a boy—I mean he didn't eat his own earwax or anything—so I swallowed and said okay. Josh nodded and went out to play kickball. All the boys were into kickball that year, the girls not so much.

When Josh left, I took a good look at the necklace. The star was gold with diamonds, except a lot of the gold had rubbed off and there were blank places where some of the diamonds used to be. It reminded me of a kid missing teeth.

I didn't tell my friends about the necklace, but after school I showed it to my mom. Was I excited? Happy? Did I think it was cool? I don't remember. But I know I didn't expect what I got, and that was a lecture. I wasn't supposed to marry anybody at least till I had finished college, she told me. I needed education and a good career. I needed to be strong and independent.

I had to give the necklace back, she said. What if it was valuable? What if Josh stole it out of his mom's jewelry box?

I don't think I had said anything up till then. I was too surprised. But of course, I had to defend Josh. The kid had asked me to marry him. He was clearly a boy with taste. So I said he was nice, not a thief, and anyway, half the diamonds were missing.

Mom said, "That's not the point."

And next thing, she was calling Dad to see what he thought. By then they had been divorced like three years, and usually they could talk without anybody yelling or crying. I didn't have to wait to hear what Dad would say. I already knew. He would go along with Mom because in general it is easier always to go along with Mom.

My first romance was toast.

I thought probably Josh would be mad the next day when I handed him the necklace at before-school recess. We were by the basketball hoop on the upper playground.

I said, "Josh, I'm not allowed to keep it. My mom."

He looked serious, but only about the same amount serious he had looked before. He took the necklace and put it in his pocket and didn't say anything. Then a basketball bounced over and hit him in the ear, and tears overflowed his brown eyes, and he had to go to the nurse.

I guess I am a wicked person because I wanted to think that he was crying not only for his ear, which had turned red, but also for lost love—me. But a week later Mimi Wong showed the same Star of David necklace to me and Amy Sutherland at lunchtime, and she told us she was going to marry Josh. I didn't say anything. Later I wondered if between when Josh gave the necklace to me and when he gave it to Mimi, he ever even took it out of his pocket.

Josh moved away when we were in fifth grade. Mimi is still around. She has had a lot of boyfriends, but I don't think she is the brightest bulb in the marquee. I haven't talked to her in probably years, but maybe sometime I'll ask her if she ever kissed Josh Silberman. Maybe that was like a beginning for her, you know? It set her off on this path of boys and kissing, while my entire romantic life was wrecked when my mom made me give back Josh Silberman's necklace.

Chapter Three

Reason Three: Because the treachery of boys knows no limits.

It takes approximately forty-eight hours for every peon at Seymour's to get the whole scoop on how Elliot and Valerie were going at it in the walk-in fridge. So when I get to work on Friday, people can't wait to rehash the juicy details with me, Jane, Victim of Heartbreak.

I survive the morning latte rush by acting all above it and cool and, "No, don't tell me. That's okay. I've forgotten all about him."

But by the prelunch lull my cool has worn off and I'm a pig soaking up juicy details and wallowing in misery.

"So Elliot goes in the walk-in for mayo, and there's Valerie, stooping to get lettuce, and like, her butt dimples, her tattoo, her pink thong—they're *all* hanging out. Elliot says it's not his fault. Elliot says he was overcome by *lust!*"

That's the gospel according to Tiffany, who wears skirts to her ankles and believes ChapStick is a sin. I can't remember what church it is she belongs to, but from the way Tiffany says it, the pastor must really get rolling when he talks to the congregation about *lust*.

"Where did you hear this?" I ask her.

"From Shuja," she says. "Loren told him."

We are waiting for bagels to come out of the toaster. It is hot in this corner behind the sandwich counter, and I can feel the sweat beads in my armpits. It is not possible that a girl could feel less attractive. I mean, who would *lust* after a girl with sweaty pits?

After lunch Arthur and I wipe down tables. He has the dish on what happened when Seymour found out.

"Seymour brought them both into his office," Arthur tells me. "Valerie immediately started to cry, said she was sorry." Arthur stops squirting and looks up at me. "Valerie's a tramp, Jane," he says, "but she's an honest tramp."

Tramp isn't the first word I personally would use to describe Valerie, but Arthur is a big fan of old black-and-white movies, the kind where "tramp" is the worst anybody'd ever say about a girl.

I don't answer, so Arthur continues: "Meanwhile, your friend Elliot first tried to deny the whole thing, which didn't make much sense after Valerie already confessed. Then Seymour gives him one more chance, says he doesn't want to lose a good employee over a single transgression—"

I can't help it—I interrupt. "Did he really say 'transgression'?"

"Seymour never forgets he used to be an English professor," Arthur says. "Do you suppose Elliot knows what it means?"

"Of course he does," I say, defending the slime bucket for no good reason except he used to be my slime bucket. "Elliot's what he is, but his vocabulary is okay. I mean, he fences."

"What does fencing have to do with it?" Arthur asks.

"Fencers have the highest IQs of any athletes. You can look it up."

Arthur's face is skeptical. "Let me guess, Jane. Elliot told you that?"

"Well, yeah," I admit. "Elliot and his mom."

Arthur shakes his head. "You do know how to pick 'em. Anyway, all he had to do to keep his job was tell the truth and apologize. But he didn't. He laid the blame on Valerie, claimed she lured him into the walk-in and grabbed him."

Elliot has not called or IM'd since it happened. Elliot is a lying weasel. Still . . . I sense this tiny little ray of light in my darkness. Before I think, I say, "Do you think that's true?"

Arthur is so disgusted, he drops his rag. *"Please."*

The tiny little ray of light goes black. I squirt the table, which by now is entirely clean and germ-free, then I wipe it furiously. "Right. So after that, what happened?"

"Well, you know how Seymour is," Arthur says. "He doesn't get mad easily, but when he's mad—watch out. He told Valerie to get back to work. Then he threw Elliot out on his ear, said he'd mail his last paycheck. Want to know more?"

"No," I say.

Arthur looks at me.

"Okay, fine," I say, "what?"

"Elliot walked half a block down the street and got a job at Panacho."

Jaws do not actually drop. This is because—and you can look this up—they are attached to cheeks. But if a jaw could drop, mine would have.

Panacho—like you don't already know—is the McDonald's of the bagel world, a giant multinational corporation with a zillion-dollar advertising budget. Seymour about had a stroke last year when Stan Zilchberg, the richest guy in town, announced his plan to open a franchise in College Springs. Stan was even a regular Seymour's customer—turkey on rye, no cheese, no mayo, extra tomatoes, and mustard.

How could he do this to us?

And there's something else, too: the annual Kickoff Parade, which is a very big deal in our very small town. Every year Seymour's Bagels wins the sweepstakes prize, commercial division, for best float. But this year there's a rumor Panacho has hired some high-powered professor at the university to build a float with special effects as good as Hollywood's. Nobody knows this for sure, though, because it's tradition that the floats remain a total secret till they're unveiled the day of the parade. Now that day is only a month away, and Seymour is so depressed, he hasn't even started planning yet.

With so little time, how can Seymour's hope to take the sweepstakes award this year?

And if Seymour's can't even beat Panacho in a float competition . . . Well, doesn't that mean Seymour's Bagels, RIP?

Anyway, as bad as I thought Elliot was before, I never thought he was bad enough to go to work for the enemy bagel store.

"That *traitor*," I say.

Chapter Four

Reason Four: Because guys have been walking out on girls since before the Flintstones.

Saturday afternoon is my weekly soda date with Grandma, when I tell her the stuff I don't tell my mom. This is because in my experience, moms are more likely to panic than grandmas are. Grandmas have seen more of the world.

Grandma and I are sitting like we always do, at the old pink Formica table in the kitchen of her condo. The sodas this week are strawberry. How you make one is, put strawberry jam, fresh strawberries, and vanilla ice cream in a blender and press the button. Let blend for thirty seconds. Turn blender off. Pour into glasses till they're halfway full. Slowly add soda water. Stir gently. Squirt whipped cream on top.

"I didn't like Elliot so much," Grandma says, "but I don't suppose that's any consolation."

"This is so weird," I say. "Now that he's history, everybody's telling me they didn't like him. You. Arthur. John. . . ."

"Your mother," Grandma adds. "You have talked to your mother about this, haven't you?"

"I told her. She was home for about five minutes yesterday. She's working on some grant, and she went out for dinner, too."

Grandma perks up. "She did?"

"Don't get too excited. They went to the Groundhog Inn, which usually means it's a work deal."

Grandma says, "Damn." Ever since she got together with Bruce, she's been hoping Mom will find a boyfriend, too. Before that, she didn't mention it so much.

"Anyway," I say, "I already knew Mom didn't like Elliot. I mean, *she*'s one of the reasons we were even having a fight."

"Your mother is?"

I sigh. "Well, kind of. It doesn't matter now." Even if Grandma is not the type to panic, I am not eager to turn all tell-all about the intimate—or maybe the word should be *gruesome*—details of what happened between Elliot and me. I know Grandma was young once. I just don't believe she remembers. Besides, weren't things different then?

Grandma doesn't press it. "I didn't like the way Elliot treated you, Jane," she says. "Men are a lot of trouble, and they have to be worth the trouble. That's how you tell if they are—by how they treat you."

Some part of me wants to defend Elliot. Didn't he bring me an almost unbroken seashell from his weekend at the Jersey shore? Didn't he tell me I was cute even when my face was breaking out? Didn't he buy me dessert? Show up on time for the prom? Go for walks even when he was tired out from fencing practice?

He did all that—and then we had a fight, and he dumped me in the nastiest possible way. So why would I defend him?

"Elliot," Grandma goes on—not helping matters any—"always acted like he was rather superior." She tilts her nose in the air in case I missed her point.

I think about this. I guess I just thought he *was* superior. Tall, blond, and handsome. Athletic, smart, brave. If you had a list for Mr. Perfect, you could have checked all the boxes.

I feel the twinge a person feels when her eyeballs are trying to wring the last drop out of her tear ducts. But I am sick of crying. I change the subject. "Is that why you like Bruce?" I say. "Because he treats you well?"

Bruce is the guy who shares Grandma's condo. They are shacked up is what my mom says, always followed by an eye roll and, "I only wish they'd get married." But I don't care if they're not married. I like Bruce. He shows this tendency to stick around rather than to bail, which is unusual in a man. Right now he's at the hardware store. He usually goes to the hardware store when I come over on Saturday afternoon. He says he's giving us privacy for our "girl talk."

"Bruce treats me like a queen," Grandma says. "Besides that, he's a good lover."

I blush right through to my backbone. *"Grandma!"*

She shrugs and says I'm as bad as my mother. "I'm not dead yet, in case you didn't notice. I still eat dessert, too." She slurps the last of her soda bubbles through the straw, making noise the way a little kid does. If Mom were here, she'd give Grandma a *look,* which is one reason Mom is not so often invited to come and have a soda.

I want to get past this *lover* stuff, so I ask the first question that pops into my head. It's about ancient history. "Is that what happened with Grandfather? He didn't treat you well?"

Most of my friends have at least four grandparents. Till Bruce showed up, though, I only had three. That's because my grandfather has never been more than a blur in our family history. There aren't any pictures. He left my grandmother when she was pregnant with my mom— Mom's an only child—and Grandma raised my mom by herself.

She was an OR nurse—OR stands for operating room. It means you see blood and gore all day, clean up after it, too. Sometimes people die right in front of you. They're all cut open—pulsing, raw, and helpless—and you're trying to save them, but some of them die. She says being a nurse like that makes you tough, but I think Grandma was already tough.

Now she laughs, which makes her earrings shake. Grandma has very short silver hair and wears earrings the size of poker chips. "I want to say he wasn't around long enough for me to find out," she says. "But I guess that's answer enough, isn't it?"

A long time ago I said something to my mom about growing up without a dad. She looked so sad I didn't bring it up again. I have never felt brave enough to say anything to Grandma, but today I do. Does surviving heartbreak give you courage?

"What was my grandfather like?" I ask. "I can't even remember his first name."

"Neither can I," she says.

"Grandma?"

18

She smiles. "A joke," she says. "It was Frank—he was named after FDR. He was a doctor. That must be where you and your mom get your smarts. He was good-looking, and he listened when I talked. In those days most doctors thought nurses were essentially field hands, but he wasn't like that. I fell for him."

"So why did you split up?" I ask.

"He was married," she says.

My heart thumps. I think I must have heard her wrong. This is my *grandmother* talking. "You mean not to *you*?" I ask.

Grandma looks at me like, what are you dumb or something. "I thought you knew that," she says. "You didn't know that?"

"How would I know that?"

"I thought I told you, or your mom must've. It's a thousand years ago now. And I turned lemons to lemonade, didn't I? Raised a lovely and successful daughter who is raising lovely, successful you."

"And all the people you took care of . . . when you were a nurse," I say, thinking out loud. "You saved them. The ones that didn't die, I mean."

Grandma nods. "Candidate for sainthood, that's me. Such a shame we're not Catholic."

Chapter Five

Reason Five: Because worthless as he is, you know that you have to be the one person on earth who is even more worthless, because he dumped you and not the other way around.

"It is not easy to get to be a saint," Amy says. Unlike my grandma and me, she *is* Catholic, and she used to have to go to these classes called CCD to get better at it. "There's this whole beatification process first," Amy goes on. "It takes years—centuries sometimes."

"I think Jane's grandma was kidding," Stacy says.

"I *know* she was kidding," Amy says. "I am just providing information. Like Jane always says—you can look it up."

Stacy, Amy, and I have been best friends so long that we count on each other for certain things. It's almost like we've each got an assignment. Usually, mine is to be the reliable one, the one who knows stuff like how many miles it is to the moon (240,000) and who was president during the 1950s (Dwight Eisenhower). Stacy, also known as Dr. Stacy, gives good advice and hatches wild schemes. Amy—besides being the inventor of her own unique Amy-logic—is well-organized and good at follow-through.

Of course, sometimes—like now, when it's Amy who knows about sainthood—we trade off assignments, and that's okay, too.

It is 11:30 A.M. on Monday. Stacy, Amy, and I are in the food court at the College Springs Mall. This is how nowhere College Springs is: It only has one mall, and there are not even any tacos at the food court, only Thai, Chinese, cinnamon rolls, and burgers. Stacy's chowing down french fries for breakfast. Amy has a paper cup of tea. I just ate the last crumb of a dried-out carrot muffin.

Why we're at this nowhere mall is: I need retail therapy. It was Stacy's idea, of course. "Shopping is a well-known painkiller," she announced on the phone.

I am not so sure about this, but I read on the back of a cereal box once that if you're "in the dumps" you should "surround yourself with good friends." I have Mondays off from Seymour's, and the pool where Stacy lifeguards is closed on Monday. Amy has about two hours of freedom before Jennifer, the supermom, picks her up and drives her to her next educational and wholesome activity.

I steal one of Stacy's fries, a cold greasy one from the bottom of the cardboard thing.

"Finding out about my grandma kind of shook me up," I say. "I mean, in your head you know a grandma has been alive a long time, and she must have been doing something all that time—"

"But something *sinful?*" Amy says.

"Oh, forget you're Catholic for a sec," Stacy says. "And anyway, it's not like *you* never did anything sinful. Who stole Sue Fehrenbach's boyfriend last year?"

"I didn't *steal* him." Amy pouts.

"You sent him IMs with heart smileys for a solid month when you knew he was going out with Sue," Stacy points out.

I nod. "You did."

"That's not stealing," Amy says. "It's . . . uh . . . it's signaling availability."

Stacy and I howl.

"And anyway . . ." By now, Amy is smiling, too. "And anyway, he only went out with me for about a week, so it barely counts."

"I wonder if Sue Fehrenbach thinks it barely counts," Stacy says.

"He was a dork besides," Amy says. "Wasn't he? Come on, wasn't he? So really—I did her a favor."

Stacy shakes her head and looks at me. "Amazing. She has now convinced herself that she is a hero instead of a boy-thief. How *does* she do it?"

"Amy-logic," I say, "and I wish I had the same skill. I feel guilty *and* I'm the victim."

"What do you mean you feel *guilty?*" Amy asks.

"I don't know. I guess I feel like I did something wrong— like I deserved to get dumped."

"You mean what happened at my party?" Stacy says. "That is just sick, sick, sick, Jane. Show some self-respect, girl!"

Stacy's parents go out of town a lot, and sometimes she has parties when they're gone. We always clean up, so they don't mind—or maybe they don't even know. Anyway, she had a party two Saturdays ago. It was the last time Elliot and I went out. Elliot and I had made a plan for that night, and it

22

didn't work out, and it was my fault, and that's another reason he and I had a fight.

"I know, Stace," I tell her. "But I can't figure out if I should have . . . well . . . gone along. So I feel guilty, and then I feel confused, and they go round and round in my head like a bad song you can't get rid of."

My two best girlfriends look all sad, and then they both lean over and hug me. Stacy is skinny as a stick, so her hug is bony. Amy, as she would be happy to tell you after ten minutes' acquaintance, is a size 3 but wears a 36D bra—her hug is pillowy. Hugs turn out to be good therapy, too. But midhug, Amy says in my ear, "Uh-oh, is my hair spazzing out?"

They both drop back into their chairs.

"No, why?" Stacy asks.

"It is, isn't it?" Amy tugs on her hair, like this will straighten it. "And that guy—he's looking at me, isn't he?"

Stacy looks over her shoulder. "Maybe," she says. "Or maybe he's looking at *me*. Did you think of that?"

Amy ignores this question and says her split ends are driving her crazy, but there's no time in her schedule for a haircut. The conversation shifts. Most days I can talk hair, too, but today I'm not in the mood, and for a second I even wonder how come Amy and Stacy *are* my best girlfriends, anyway.

We have known each other since Mrs. Roeber's class, third grade, which is when Amy's family moved to College Springs. It was in sixth grade that we got close, though. Sixth grade was Mrs. Nicoletti's class, and we were doing a group project about the Battle of Gettysburg.

23

Trevor Williams and Ike Dreibelbeis were supposed to work with us, but Trevor had figured out already that if you're in a group, some people are responsible and some people aren't, and you all get the same grade. Ike did the work okay, but he was too shy to talk to girls, so his mom dropped off everything he did. Meanwhile, Amy, Stacy, and I made the exhibit together, and it was fun, and when it was done, we were so used to hanging out that we just kept on.

I still remember the first time we all went to Stacy's house. We sat on the floor of her huge bedroom and cut out photographs of Civil War heroes. Her room is different now, but in sixth grade everything in it matched—even Stacy's own pastel iMac on Stacy's own pastel desk. Her parents are both doctors, and she is the youngest kid. What this means is her parents worked so hard raising her two big sisters and got so exhausted, they are pretty much letting Stacy raise herself. One time Stacy told me her mom used to read to her sisters every night at bedtime, but she bought Stacy a TV for her room so Stacy could watch TV instead.

Stacy says this stuff like it's no big deal—it's only kind of funny. But I think it's not that funny.

Our next meeting was at Amy's house, which is less luxurious, but it's just as nice because Jennifer the supermom doesn't work for money, she stays home and works to make everything perfect for her family. Amy and her mom and dad and two little brothers actually sit in the dining room and eat dinner off of china plates, even on week nights.

When it was my turn to have Stacy and Amy over to work on the project, I was totally worried. This was back in sixth grade, remember. Mom had just gotten her first job at the college library. We were still broke. The front door needed paint. The kitchen floor was curling around the edges. Half the furniture was handed down from Grandma after Grandma moved into her condo.

I figured our old ugly sofa by itself would be enough to send Stacy and Amy screaming from my life—but when the day came and they actually rang the doorbell and walked in, it wasn't like that. The three of us sat on the floor like we were anyplace, like we were at Stacy's or Amy's really nice houses, and we drew arrows on maps Ike Dreibelbeis had found on the Internet. When we were done, Mom brought us cocoa and microwave popcorn.

I tune back in to my current life. Amy and Stacy have moved off hair and are on to Amy's new raspberry tea diet. Amy is always trying some new diet. Last year Stacy and I got worried about this, and we went to our health teacher, Mrs. Stanton, and ratted Amy out, only we called it staging an intervention.

Mrs. Stanton said: "Is Amy losing weight?"

Stacy and I said: "No."

Mrs. Stanton said: "Is Amy gaining weight?"

Stacy and I said: "No, never."

Mrs. Stanton said: "Is she sick a lot? Tired a lot?"

Stacy and I had to laugh at that. Amy's mom keeps her so busy, she isn't allowed to be either sick or tired.

"Then I think," Mrs. Stanton said, "that your friend is okay. But please check back if you see symptoms developing."

Since then, symptoms have never developed, but Stacy and I remain on the alert.

Now Stacy's cell phone rings. Amy and I look at each other. "Dr. Stacy," I mouth, and Amy nods.

Stacy yanks the phone out and looks at it. "Uh-oh," she says. Then she swivels so she's facing away from us. Amy looks at her watch. "What time's Jennifer picking you up?" I ask.

"At one," Amy says.

"What is it you have to do again?"

"Clarinet," Amy says. "The all-state summer band auditions are next week, and I'm up for first chair, only my teacher thinks I need coaching."

"You're kidding," I say. "Why didn't you tell us before?" I knew Amy was great at clarinet, but I didn't know she was that great. We're only going to be juniors and usually it's seniors who go to all-state, let alone play first chair. "That is so cool! I wish I did anything as well as you play clarinet."

"It's not such a big deal," Amy says. "I practice hours every day. It would be pathetic if I were bad. Anyway, I *hate* clarinet."

"You always say that," I tell her. "But I don't get it. Why don't you quit if you hate it?"

"I've been doing it so long, it would be stupid to quit now, with college applications coming up. Then there's my mom. . . ." She shakes her head. "Anyway, the second I get to college, that's when I quit."

"Maybe your mom needs a hobby," I say. "I mean besides you and your brothers. Maybe she should be the one taking clarinet lessons."

Amy laughs. Stacy swivels back.

"Jo's dad," she says, "is totally having fits about her getting a job at Wendy's because she totally flunked bio and is taking it in summer school, but she says she needs the money for a car, and he won't give it to her. I told her to keep the job but make sure her dad sees her studying bio."

"Jo who?" Amy asks.

"Yeah, who?" I say.

"Winchell," Stacy says. "You know her. She used to go out with Steve from the soccer team."

"Since when are you friends with her?" I say.

"She was at the pool this weekend, and we started talking," Stacy says. "I'm not sure I even like her that much. I told her to put sunscreen on her toes—it's always the toes that get it—and she didn't, and then, of course, her toes got sunburned."

"If you're not even sure you like her," I say patiently, "why are you giving her advice?"

"Because she needs me," Stacy says. "It's like I've told you before, Amy teaches Sunday school. You feed bagel sandwiches to the hungry masses. And I help people with their problems." She shrugs. "It's a community service."

"Well, today we are supposed to be helping *Jane*," Amy reminds her. "Here is my proposal: Doug Blanders. He has a *great* body."

"You guys," I say.

"Doug Blanders?" Stacy makes a face. "No offense, but this is totally why you are *not* the one in charge of advice, Amy. Doug Blanders has a nose like a blob of dough!"

"You guys," I repeat.

"You are so shallow, Stacy," Amy says. "Have you taken a good look at Doug's butt when he wears those old jeans?"

"Oh, right," Stacy says, "and your appreciation for his butt makes you deeper than me, who can't get past the raw biscuit in the middle of his face."

"You guys!"

Amy and Stacy look at me like for a minute they had forgotten I was here.

"Who says I'm even interested in another boy?" I say.

"Think about it, Jane," Stacy says. "What do you do when your old dog dies? You get a puppy. This is the same thing."

I want to tell Stacy she is annoying. This is *not* the same thing. My heart is broken. I feel about one eyelash away from total blubbering meltdown every second of every day.

I want to say, *Don't you guys get it?*

But I don't say that, because I know they do.

I guess right now, being cheered up by my best friends is just another thing I have to suffer through.

Amy and Stacy are arguing about which is better, a boy or a puppy.

"Did we come here to shop or not?" I ask.

Amy waves her empty cup in a pretend toast: "To shop!"

"To shop!" Stacy and I echo. Then—one for all, and all for one—we advance into the dinky and pathetic College Springs Mall.

Chapter Six

Reason Six: Because if you have a butt like a tomato, retail therapy won't fix your broken heart.

"Why do we have to go to U.S. Canary, anyway?" I ask. "Why can't we go to Abel and Crum, or even Canyon?"

"Because this year everyone is shopping at U.S. Canary," says Amy.

"*Duh,*" says Stacy.

"Who makes these decisions?" I ask. "Some girl in Texas? Some girl in Beverly Hills? We're like lemmings, for gosh sakes."

"I'm pretty sure lemmings still shop at Abel and Crum," Stacy says.

"Funny," I say.

"The point is nobody wants to look like a dork," Amy says, and I have to admit she's right about that—especially if, like me, you're afraid deep down that you really *are* a dork.

Inside U.S. Canary, Stacy assigns Amy and me each a rack and says, "Go!" I tug a hundred hangers and find nothing, but in five minutes Stacy and Amy hand me an armload of capris, jeans, skirts, and tops. They look so happy about it, too, like who could think about your wreck of a romantic life—or your grandma's startling revelation—when there are clothes to try on?

So I try to get in the spirit, and I collect my number from the guard of the dressing rooms, and I hide behind the flimsy curtain and strip down to my underwear—and of course, I do my best not to see so much as a single goose pimple of my fluorescent-lit flesh in the mirror. I already know, thank you a lot, that I am pale and bulgy.

The clothes Stacy and Amy handed me look perfectly fine on the hangers, and supposedly they are my size, and when I stare at the various Janes in the mirror, some of them who look back look okay.

But when I turn around to check my rear in the mirror, oh *horror.*

I have to take some serious deep breaths and make a deal with God that I will take up marathon running tomorrow, I swear, because I have a butt like a tomato.

I put the clothes back on hangers and walk out, and Stacy and Amy are waiting.

Amy says, "You didn't even show us!"

I tell her my butt looks like a tomato.

"You have a nice butt!" Stacy says. "I'm sure everything looks great!"

I look at Stacy's butt, which, essentially, does not exist. I look at Amy's, which takes up the same amount of space as two plump apples.

Amy says, "Come on, Jane, you have a bad self-image. Now go back in there and put on whatever you liked best and come back out and show us. We'll tell the truth. Honest."

I do. And when I show them, they look at each other and agree to get me more clothes to try on—so see?

"Forget it, you guys," I say. "Anyway, this stuff is too expensive. If I don't buy it, I'm saving ten hours of bagel wages."

"Who cares about money?" Stacy says, which when your parents are both doctors and are too tired to read their credit card statements carefully is easy to say.

Amy says, "Just give us one more chance, Jane."

And they leave and come back with more clothes.

"This skirt is roomy," Amy says.

"What about this T-shirt with the ruffle?" Stacy asks.

I go back into the torture chamber—dressing room, I mean. The orange capris Stacy found—surprise—are a disaster. Add a stem and some leaves, and I could enter the fruit-and-vegetable pageant. But Amy is right about the roomy skirt, and the ruffle T-shirt. Do I really like them? Or am I just so sick of trying on clothes that anything would be good?

Stacy and Amy are all of a sudden like my own personal cheerleaders when they see how I look in the skirt and top. I am beautiful, they say. I am a knockout. I am a boy magnet.

I say, all sarcastic, "Yeah, yeah, yeah."

But really I feel pretty good, pretty happy, for about ten minutes—long enough to get out my wallet and pay. I mean, for right then, I actually kind of believe them.

And I guess maybe this answers the question of why they're my best friends at all.

Chapter Seven

Reason Seven: Because when you least expect it, you will start thinking in the back of your brain about your worthless, slimy toad of an ex-boyfriend who just dumped loser you, and you could even start to cry all over again, which is humiliating.

On Tuesday I leave my house a few minutes early for work. I am walking by Ashok's house when he calls me from his garage. Ashok has been my next-door neighbor since we were babies drooling on blankets. Our moms used to take us to the park, and we would play in the sandbox. One time I told him, "Good castle," and he said, "It's not a castle. It's a particle accelerator."

So now you know what Ashok is like. I get good grades because I do everything I'm supposed to. Ashok gets good grades because if you're a genius, you can't help it.

The door to Ashok's garage is open, but it's dark and I can't see very well, so I walk closer and finally make out Ashok's shape kneeling on the concrete. Next to him is some kind of metal pipe attached to a motor. The nozzle on the pipe is aimed at a white sheet the size of poster board, that's supported by a metal bracket.

"Is it a particle accelerator?" I ask.

He laughs, but then his face turns serious. "Jane, I just wanted to tell you—I am so sorry about my mother."

Looked at one way, it's Ashok's mom who's responsible for Elliot dumping me. Last week she mentioned to my mom that

I got home after my curfew, which got me grounded. If I hadn't been grounded . . . well, Elliot and I might not have had a fight, and if we hadn't had a fight, maybe Valerie wouldn't have looked quite so attractive? Mrs. Bose is famous for putting her foot in her mouth. I don't think she meant to get me in trouble, but with Mrs. Bose it's hard to tell.

"I won't blame you for your mom," I say, "if you won't blame me for mine." I nod at his contraption. "So seriously, what is that thing?"

"Do you want a demonstration?" he asks.

"Depends. Is it dangerous?"

He laughs. "Not as dangerous as my mother." He flips a switch on the motor, which revs like a motorcycle, then quiets to a hum. "Keep your fingers crossed, Jane," he says. Then he puts a heavy work glove on his right hand, takes hold of the pipe, and aims the nozzle.

I expect water to spray out, but what actually happens is a lot more exciting. It's *fire* that shoots from the pipe and hits the white sheet. The garage begins to heat up, but for about thirty seconds nothing happens to the sheet at all. There's not even a black mark on it. Ashok looks at his watch and smiles, but then, all of a sudden—*poof*—the sheet glows blinding orange, turns black, then turns to smoke.

Ashok turns off the motor, lays down the nozzle, and looks at the tidy little pile of ashes in front of him on his garage floor. "Oh, dear," he says.

"Oh, dear," I say, too, and then I burst into tears.

"Jane!" Ashok bounces up like he's spring-loaded. "What is it? Do you think this was your fault? Believe me, it

33

was not! It is some problem with the material! It is entirely *my* fault!"

Ashok looks around desperately and feels in his pockets. "I have no Kleenex!" he says, and his voice is so full of despair, it makes me smile, and I get a grip.

"I'll be fine," I say. "It wasn't really the fire. It's just that lately, I'm kind of . . . uh . . . fragile. And I guess something burning up—it's dumb, but maybe it seemed sort of symbolic?"

"Can I do anything, Jane? Anything at all?" he asks.

I shake my head, sniff back the last tear. "I'll be fine," I repeat. "So what's all this for, anyway?"

Ashok looks at the pile of ashes again. "Professor LeCert asked me to experiment with some lightweight, malleable, fireproof materials," he says. "He didn't explain the ultimate purpose, or . . ."—he scratches his head—"perhaps he did, and I forgot."

"That sounds like you, Ashok."

"I know," he says. "My father says I need to live more on Planet Earth and less on Planet Ashok."

Ashok's father is a chemical engineering professor. So is his mom. They came here from India when Ashok was a baby. At winter break they always "go home," and my mom and I water the plants for them.

Ashok looks up at me and smiles. His smile takes me by surprise. It is beautiful. For a second I almost forget he's just Ashok. "How is your job going, Jane?" he asks. "Your mom told my mom you are putting in almost forty hours per week."

It would be uncool to describe the joys of making bagel sandwiches, espresso drinks, and smoothies to the Hindu

34

Benjamin Franklin. I mean, what does he care? I ought to just say it's okay in a tone that implies that working at Seymour's Bagels is beneath my (still undiscovered) talents.

But instead, I tell Ashok the truth. I like working at Seymour's. I like Seymour. I like the other peons. I like having a paycheck with my name on it. I like watching my bank account grow. I like knowing which espresso drink is which—macchiato, latte, cappuccino, Americano.

Ashok says, "I'm glad for you," then he looks back at the pile of ashes on the garage floor. When he gets this light-weight, malleable, fireproof invention of his perfected, he'll probably win a Nobel Prize for it. Meanwhile, I'll be perfecting my milk-frothing technique. Is it possible in all the world that there's anybody who's as big a loser as me?

Chapter Eight

Reason Eight: Because boys have cooties, which are not the same as germs, or else they wouldn't have a separate name. A cootie is actually a microscopic magnetized particle. Each individual cootie is weak, but if you get too close to a major cootie source, you could become trapped in a cootie force field. This is why it is advisable to keep a ten-foot safety zone between yourself and major cootie sources—e.g., boys—at all times.

The first day I ever laid eyes on Elliot Badgi was Saturday, March 18, just a little over four months ago. He was carrying a vat of cream cheese on his shoulder, but broad as they were, his shoulders weren't the immediate attraction. That was his voice, which is deep and resonant. And his eyes, which are sort of hot and blue at the same time. Oh—and his hair, which is blond, shiny, and floppy, like the hair in a magazine ad for conditioner.

Anyway, on that Saturday I had only been working at Seymour's Bagels for two weeks, but really, I'd been hanging around the place my whole life. Seymour used to be an English professor at the college, but about twenty years ago he got sick of grading papers and decided his true destiny was to bring bagels to central Pennsylvania. This doesn't sound like a big deal now, when you can buy bagels at any supermarket and Panacho advertises them on TV 24-7, but back then in this nowhere town, it was practically a food revolution.

Seymour makes his bagels the way you're supposed to: boiling them first, then baking them. That's why they're chewy and delicious, so of course, they caught on. And after a while he added espresso and smoothies and scones and fancy sandwiches with real stinky cheeses instead of the tasteless orange Play-Doh slices most places use. Without Seymour's, my mom says, College Springs would still be in the Dark Ages foodwise.

So when I turned sixteen and my mom said I should start earning my own spending money, it was obvious that the first place I'd apply was Seymour's.

Mostly, I like working there, but there are some bad things, like how the smell of pickles and onions stays in your nose forever after you work the sandwich counter, and like how your feet hurt at the end of a long shift, and like Witch Lady.

Witch Lady's real name is Andrea, and she is the manager. I think she is probably about thirty-five, but it's hard to tell. Her hair is dark and straight, and hangs down her back and into her eyes. She wears her Seymour's T-shirt and jeans in this grocery-bag way, like she's afraid to reveal that a female body lurks underneath. It is possible that inside her someplace there is a nice person, but we peons can't find her. I have never seen Witch Lady smile.

When you come in to cover your shift at Seymour's, the first thing you do is check in with Witch Lady in her office. On Saturday, March 18, I arrived on time—2:25 for my 2:30 shift. Witch Lady looked at her watch and said, "Punctual," but I had a feeling what she really meant was, "Too bad you made it. I was thinking how much fun it would be to fire you."

There is a mirror in Witch Lady's office so employees can do a face check. According to the Seymour's employee handbook, "Good grooming is essential in the food service industry. No one wishes to eat a sandwich that has been handled by a person with foreign matter on his teeth or untidiness about the ears and nostrils." The reason, if you're wondering, that I can quote from memory the Seymour's handbook is because Arthur knows chunks of it by heart and likes to spout them like poetry. Seymour pretends to get mad at Arthur for this, but actually, I think he likes it.

I did my face check. Nothing foreign about the teeth, ears, or nostrils. I washed my hands. Then I said to Witch Lady, "Where do you want me?" And Witch Lady said, "Why don't you relieve Tiff at the register? I think she's done about as much addition as she can be expected to do in one day."

This wasn't a very nice thing to say. Maybe Tiffany isn't the brightest person who ever made change for a roast beef and cheddar, but she works hard. Does Witch Lady mean to be so nasty? Or maybe she just can't help it?

But now we get to the critical and disastrous moment—the moment when I heard from behind me this guy voice I didn't recognize, and the voice said, "Very funny."

Don't ask me why, but the second I heard that voice, I stood up straight. What was the deal with that, anyway? It was like the voice reverberated around inside my rib cage. Crazier still, I had the feeling before I turned around that I knew what the voice's source would look like, and what he would look like was good.

I turned around. I saw him. And—oh, oncoming heartbreak—I was right.

Chapter Nine

Reason Nine: Because a boy who comes to the rescue is not necessarily a hero.

The source of the voice was Elliot, but you knew that, right? Besides the eyes and the hair and the shoulders, he was tall, with a long, straight nose and good cheekbones. He had dandy eyelashes, which is just so unfair. If I don't have time to curl mine, they look like nothing.

"You shouldn't be so hard on Tiffany," Elliot told Witch Lady, which fooled me momentarily into thinking he was a nice guy. But then he added, "You shouldn't be hard on any of the hired help, in fact. Take this one here. What's her name?"

Elliot's voice and then his looks had provoked this nice goosefleshy feeling in me. But "hired help"? And "this one here"? Yuck! So much for gooseflesh.

Witch Lady said this-is-Jane/this-is-Elliot. He had just come up from the basement, which is why the cream cheese vat was balanced on his shoulder. He seemed huge. His smile was bright. But I was irritated, so I imagined his teeth covered with foreign matter—green, *slimy* foreign matter—and I said, all cold, "Hi," and before he could answer, I turned and walked away.

Elliot watched me go. I don't know how I knew this, but I did. Let him look, I thought. I don't care how big he thinks my butt is. He is an arrogant jerk.

At the register I told Tiffany that she could go work the pastry counter—usually the easiest job at Seymour's— and she said, the way she does, "Praise the Lord," which she sincerely means.

It was your basic afternoon shift at Seymour's. I rang up baguettes and bagels and sandwiches and smoothies. I wiped down the counter and straightened the creamers and the sugar packets and the coffee stirrers. Elliot scooped cream cheese out of the giant vat into smaller tubs while he talked to Valerie, tattoo queen, who was working at the sandwich counter. Valerie grinned and fluttered the way girls like Valerie do.

I had started to think about going home and what I'd be doing that night—whether Stacy and Amy were busy or might want to hang out—when I felt a draft that meant the front door had opened. I looked out the window, and it had started raining. Then I heard Tiff—the pastry counter is by the front door—say, "Hi, Mr. Black," and I turned and saw him come in.

Mr. Black was somebody I saw around a lot—on the sidewalk, in the library, at the park—but I didn't know where he lived or anything. He seemed pretty old, with a gray mustache and a bald head. That day he wasn't wearing a raincoat, and his clothes were damp. I had seen him in Seymour's before, but I never saw him cause trouble. Valerie has worked at Seymour's a long time, though, and from the way she acted, she expected something. She nudged Elliot, and he said, "Shoot."

Mr. Black said, "Tiffany. Have I got that right?"

Tiffany always sticks to the perfect-employee script the way it's written in the handbook. She said, "That's right, sir. What may I get for you?"

Mr. Black said, "Still got those raisin bagels?" and the way he said *raisin*, it was more like you'd say *cockroach*.

Tiffany said, "Yes, Mr. Black."

"And blueberry?"

Tiffany said, "Yes, Mr. Black."

"Chocolate chip? Sun-dried tomato?"

Tiffany said, "Yes, Mr. Black."

"What about whole wheat? You still carry whole wheat?"

By then, even Seymour would have forgiven an employee for getting annoyed. But Tiffany really buys that turn-the-other-cheek stuff. She said, "We carry a lot of varieties, sir."

Mr. Black said, "Phooey!" and he might as well have spit. Was Mr. Black like crazy or something? I almost thought he was going to hit Tiffany. I thought of going for Witch Lady, but then I remembered she had gone home with a headache. While I stood there indecisive, paralyzed, Elliot moved. All quick and quiet he circled through espresso and past smoothies till he was behind Tiffany and facing Mr. Black.

"May I help you, sir?" Elliot asked.

Tiffany breathed again, and so did I. Unfortunately, something else happened. My heart stuttered. Protecting Tiffany that way, Elliot didn't look like an arrogant jerk anymore.

"The bagel is a noble food," Mr. Black said. "People have been eating bagels for thousands of years. The egg bagel. The salt bagel. The poppy-seed bagel. All noble foods. Foods with

41

a history. But this!" He pointed at the date nut bagels. "This is an abomination!"

Elliot said, "I'm sorry you feel that way, sir."

Mr. Black said, "And I am personally affronted that your boss, Mr. Seymour Smarty-Pants, who should know better, would sell them."

"Can I get you a dozen poppy-seed bagels then, sir?" Elliot asked.

Tiffany pulled out a paper bag and opened it.

"How could I in good conscience line the pockets of a man like this?" Mr. Black asked. "A man who contributes to the decline of civilization as we know it? A man who corrupts young people such as yourselves by putting sugar and even chocolate in a bagel and then expecting you, with no experience of history, to sell those bagels? To do his dirty work for him?"

"You are absolutely right," Elliot said. "How about a dozen bagels on the house?"

I turned my head so Mr. Black wouldn't see me smile. Elliot's offer probably sounded generous, but it was only an hour till we closed and the guy from the food bank came to take the leftovers, anyway.

Mr. Black didn't answer for a minute, and in that minute I noticed the hole in the elbow of his sweater and how his clothes hung loose on him. He pretty much looked like a food bank customer himself. I felt kind of bad, but being old and poor doesn't give you the right to go around bullying peons at a bagel store, does it?

"They're probably stale," Mr. Black said.

Tiffany, loyal employee, said, "We don't sell stale bagels."

Elliot said, "Made out at our production facility this morning, but I'd be happy to give you a dozen. We won't tell Seymour." Elliot winked at Mr. Black, which turned out to be a genius move on Elliot's part because apparently Mr. Black now decided it would be cool to put something over on a guy who wanted to bring down civilization by selling blueberry bagels.

"Poppy seed then," Mr. Black said, "and it's a baker's dozen, correct? So make the thirteenth an egg bagel."

Tiffany dropped an egg bagel on top of the others and handed the bag over. Even she was out of patience by then and didn't smile, but Elliot did: "Have a good day!"

An instant later the door clicked, and Mr. Black was safely on the sidewalk. Elliot looked over at me, still smiling. I tried to stay calm by clinging to the thought of what a jerk he was, by imagining green, slimy foreign matter oozing from his nostrils. It didn't work, though. My calm was all undone after about one second, and I smiled back, and time stopped, and for approximately ever we were locked in this look that I could feel, I hate to tell you, shooting right up and down me, hair to toenails and all points between.

Chapter Ten

Reason Ten: Because romance can be very very stressful.

Elliot's shift must have ended before mine because I looked around when I was getting ready to go, and he was gone. He had left without even a wave good-bye.

So there I was, all crushed and thinking I must have totally misunderstood that eye-lock—until I walked out the door to go home and he was waiting beside an expired parking meter in the drizzle.

He said, "Can I walk you? I think I live by you, more or less." Later I found out Elliot actually lives with his mom over by Paterno Park. He only claimed he lived near me because he thought I might be *interesting*, that was the word he used, and he wanted an excuse to walk me home. It was like a month before he told me this, and of course, I was all flattered—even more when I realized he had walked a mile out of his way in the rain for *me*. This was the kind of thing that happened to Amy and Stacy, never to me.

"I didn't bring an umbrella," I said.

"Me neither," he said. "Anyway, some people think it's romantic to walk in the rain."

Wow, I thought. Did he really say that?

He started walking down Main Street, and I fell in with him. We passed Panacho, which wasn't open yet, but the sign with the famous green and yellow Panacho dragon was in the window. I said my mom and I were worried about Seymour's staying in business after Panacho opened, and Elliot said he wasn't.

"Have you ever had their bagels? They're more like hamburger buns!" he said.

Then he told me he'd been working at Seymour's for a year, that I didn't see him around school because he went to Zeta, which is like this alternative high school. Arthur went there freshman year, but he transferred back to College Springs High because our drama teacher is better.

"How come you go to Zeta?" I asked. I always associated it with oddball kids—and believe me, Arthur qualifies—or with the intellectual ones who wear black and smoke clove cigarettes. Elliot didn't smell like cigarettes at least.

"Fencing," he said. "I have to train all the time, travel a lot. The school stuff has to be flexible, and Zeta is. Some days I only have two classes."

"And you work, too," I said.

"No choice," he said. "The team's expensive; the gear's expensive. My mom's a lawyer, but my parents are divorced. We're not rich."

"My parents are divorced, too," I tell him. "Since I was like three years old. My dad lives in Pleasant Haven. He's a teacher."

"What about your mom?" Elliot asked.

"She works in the library at the university," I said. "Actually, she just got a promotion, something called an endowed

45

chair. It's kind of a big deal." I looked up to see if he thought I was bragging. If he did, it didn't show on his face; but I still felt embarrassed I'd mentioned it, so I added, "She's worked really hard to get that job. I guess I'm kind of proud of her."

"Cool," he said. "My mom and I get along good, too."

I almost told him being proud of your mom is not the same as getting along with her, but this seemed like a lot to explain, so I asked if he had brothers and sisters.

He shook his head. "You?"

"Uh-uh," I said. "I guess we have a lot in common." As soon as I said that, I felt embarrassed again, like it was too aggressive, so I sneaked another glance at his face. He was smiling. *Oh my gosh, was he ever good-looking.*

We turned off Main Street and walked up Nance, past the fraternity houses and a couple of student rentals, where last fall's leaves, now soggy and matted, still littered the front yards. I started to feel like somebody should say something, so I asked about Mr. Black. "Does he come in a lot? You really handled that whole thing well. I was almost scared of him."

"Thanks," Elliot said. "I guess I'm kind of brave that way. With people, I mean. My mom says all I need is a cape and I'd be a superhero."

"Your mom says *that*? Wow—the two of you really do get along good."

"It's like a joke," Elliot said. "I mean, obviously. It goes with the fencing."

"I get it," I said. "So Mr. Black must be the nefarious villain. But who is he, anyway?"

"I think he knows Seymour or something," Elliot said. "I've seen them talking before. It's only lately he's on this bagels-end-of-the-world thing. Maybe he's getting crazy. But I can handle him. No problem."

I kind of half smiled. Was Elliot showing off for me? I flashed on the image of a peacock fanning its tail.

"I'll ask my grandma about Mr. Black," I said. "She knows everybody. She was a nurse at the hospital, so she even knows about their insides."

"That's gross," Elliot said. Then he looked down at me for several steps, and I worried about my hair because it was damp and flat, and I worried about my Seymour's T-shirt because it was starting to cling. Luckily, I was wearing one of the bras my mom gave me—so respectable, it's practically armor-plated. Otherwise, I would have looked like the loser in a wet T-shirt contest.

When we turned the corner onto Irving Avenue, my street, Ashok's mom's car went past us, then she turned into their driveway, and she and Ashok climbed out. When Elliot and I got closer, I could hear that they were arguing.

"But I *must* get my driver's license!" Ashok said.

"Why?" his mom said. "I drive you wherever you need to go."

"I am almost grown!" Ashok said. "I should not be relying on my mother so much."

"Why not?" his mother said. "You should consider yourself fortunate that—" She had been pulling groceries from the trunk, but now she looked up and saw Elliot and me. "Hello, Jane!" she called. "Who is your young man?"

47

This was a classic Neena Bose foot-in-mouth remark.

"*Mother!*" Ashok said.

Mrs. Bose looked from him to me, totally innocent, and said, "What? Is he *not* your young man, Jane? So sorry. My mistake. At any rate, it is a rare pleasure to see you. I miss the days when you and Ashok dressed up and played tea party together. You were such a darling little girl—that healthy round belly and those blond ringlets! How is your mother?"

Ashok's mom was clearly going for a record here—maximum humiliation in minimum words. I sucked in a breath, let it out slowly, and said, "My mother is fine, Mrs. Bose. Hi, Ashok."

Ashok said, "Hi, Jane," but something about the way he said it included a silent "I am so sorry about my idiot mother."

"And who *is* your young man, Jane?" Mrs. Bose asked. "That is to say, who is this young man you are walking with? I don't believe I know him."

I introduced Elliot and explained we knew each other from Seymour's. Elliot never had to say anything except "Hey." Finally we escaped. I looked back, and Ashok was trailing his mother into the house. They were still having an intense conversation, but Ashok was carrying groceries and couldn't use his hands. He was wagging his head, instead.

Elliot walked me up to my front door. I don't know what I expected. It's not like we'd been out together and he was going to kiss me or something. I was thinking maybe I should invite him to come in—only the Very-Nice guys were working on the downstairs, so this was kind of a problem—but before I even finished that thought, he said, "Gotta go. Junk to do."

He put his hands in his pockets and turned to walk away.

I felt kind of like I'd just flunked a math test I thought I'd aced. I mean, apparently, my calculations were wrong. But then he turned back toward me, and walking backward, he said, "Want to go out for dessert? Tomorrow? Tivoli is good—over in Belletoona? I can pick you up—like at eight?"

I said, "Sure, yeah," and it was a good thing I don't have a tail, because I would have wagged it like a puppy with its eye on a Milk-Bone.

Chapter Eleven

Reason Eleven: Because boys are time-consuming.

Inside, I caught a whiff of fresh paint.

"Hello?" I called. "Mom?"

It was John who answered. "'Lo, Janey."

I followed his voice and found him painting the guest bathroom by the stairs. Mom had picked out a shade of green she called wintergreen, but it looked more like cold medicine to me. "Your mom's gone to the paint store again," John went on. "She'll be back in a few minutes. Who was that good-looking kid, anyway? New friend o' yours?"

Oh, great. First Mrs. Bose, now John. Couldn't a girl get any privacy?

"How did you even see him from in here?" I asked.

"I got X-ray vision," John said, "like all parents. You oughta get a towel and dry your hair—you'll catch pneumonia."

"You worry too much," I said.

"Like all parents," he repeated. "You and that boy keeping company or just walking in the rain?"

If Mom or Dad asked me a question that direct, I'd probably be annoyed, but with John I didn't mind so much. Maybe that's because I didn't think he cared about the answer so much. "For now," I said, "it's just walking in the rain. But isn't he gorgeous?"

The floor of the bathroom was covered with paint-spattered canvas. John was down there painting above the baseboard with tiny brushstrokes. He hadn't taped first. He didn't need to. John is a really good painter. As far as I can tell, he's good at everything he does.

"*Gorgeous?*" he said. "I thought you told me you weren't interested in boys."

"I did?"

"Your exact words were, 'Why waste my time on boys when I could be earning money or studying to get into a good college?'"

"I said that?"

John dipped his brush. "Day before yesterday."

"Hmm," I said. "Well, day before yesterday I hadn't met Elliot."

John laughed. "You know, Jane—if you don't mind my saying so—"

My turn to laugh. "You're gonna say so anyway."

"Ain't that the truth?" He leaned back to look at the wall. "If you don't mind my saying so, you work too hard. Kids your age—you're supposed to be having *fun*. Get the homework done, sure, but then cut loose a little."

"You sound like my dad," I said. "He thinks I'm too ambitious. He says, 'Whaddaya wanna be, a brain surgeon?'"

John let the brush drip paint into the can and looked up at me. "You want to be a brain surgeon?"

"I have no clue what I want to be," I said. "Something important. Something special. Brain surgeon would be okay. Only I'm not so sure about the blood. A judge maybe? The mayor of a big city?"

"What about first lady?" John said.

"What about president?" I said.

"If you want to be president, how come you're not a class officer or somethin'?"

"It's a big popularity contest at my school," I said. "They never do anything."

John looked up at me. "Well, if you were one of them, you could be the one that did do something. Ever think of that?"

"Yeah," I said. "I have thought of that. You want to know the truth?"

He didn't look at me, just went back to painting. "Truth is good."

I shrugged. "I'm afraid I'll lose. I don't want to lose."

"Heck, Janey," John said. "You gotta lose sometimes. Otherwise you don't appreciate it when you win."

I thought about that a minute. "If I was a class officer," I said, "I'd have even less time for fun. Did you think of that?"

John wagged the paintbrush at me. "You might have fun being a class officer." He shrugged his shoulders in turn, like they hurt. "These bones are too old for crawling around on the floor."

"You're not old," I said—which is the same thing I tell my grandma, and she *is* old. "Uh . . . how old are you? Can I ask?"

"Forty-two," John said. "My birthday's in December if you want to get me something."

"What did you want to be—when you were in high school?" I asked.

"Down on the floor painting bathrooms," he said.

"You did?"

John laughed again, and I felt dumb. "Oh—you were kidding."

"I was and I wasn't," he said. "I wanted what I got—have a house, raise a family. I wasn't too particular about the ways and means. Turned out I have a knack for this kind of work."

"Do you like it?" I asked.

"Sure," he said. "Sometimes. I don't like yelling at suppliers and subs when they're lazy-butt late. I do like seeing a job come together—results that look good and make the client happy. Painting isn't bad. Quick gratification and no heavy lifting."

"At school they're always telling us we have to have a career plan," I said. "It's like we're supposed to know right now what classes we'll take in business school or else we'll end up washing dishes."

"And what's wrong with washing dishes?" John said. "So long as you do a good job at it. So long as you like it. What about your friends? What do they want?"

"They're more focused than me," I said. "Stacy's going to be a psychiatrist. Arthur wants to be a costumer on Broadway. And Amy—she's got it narrowed down to anything but clarinet player."

John wiped his hands on his pants, stood up, stretched. He had a spot of green paint on his cheek and a few green highlights in his hair. "Janey, you're sixteen, in case you hadn't noticed. You wanna know what I think?"

"You're gonna tell me whether I do or not," I said.

John nodded. "What I think is, there's plenty of time yet for plenty of things—for winning, for losing . . . even for boys."

Plenty of time for boys?

John had that wrong. The next day it took me about three hours just to get dressed to eat dessert with Elliot, plus there were two phone calls to Amy and four to Stacy for advice, not to mention IMing.

I also walked downtown and bought myself something I had always wanted but had never owned—an eyelash curler. Till then I had always been afraid something would go wrong and all my eyelashes would be decapitated. There I'd be, looking down into the bathroom sink, and in it would be all these teensy tiny hairs, and in horror I would realize they were once attached to my eyelids and no product manufactured would ever glue them back.

But having an actual date made me feel brave, and after all, if eyelash curlers were dangerous, wouldn't they be banned by the federal government?

The eyelash curler I bought cost five dollars, which is about forty-five minutes of making bagel sandwiches or smoothies at Seymour's. When I tried it out, I did not decapitate anything, but I did pinch my eyelid a couple of times. In the end, though—guess what! Eyelash curlers work!

At 7:45—after all that advice from Stacy and Amy—I put on my favorite jeans and a long-sleeve T-shirt with daisies embroidered on it. Stacy suggested the T-shirt because the daisies looked cheerful and also would "correct my proportions," which means make my boobs look bigger, so they come close to balancing out my rear end.

At five till eight I came down the stairs, lipstick on, eyelashes styled—totally ready to go. Mom was still on the phone with John from Very-Nice. There were critical decisions to make about the downstairs bathroom, like switch plates and faucets and towel bars, and I am telling you, there is *nothing* more boring than remodeling a house. Come to think of it, Mom had been on the phone with John all through dinner, too.

When I was little, Mom and I used to eat together almost every night, even if it was just canned tomato soup and grilled cheese. Lately, the food is better—like we eat takeout Chinese from the expensive place and pizza from the place that has a brick oven—but she and I don't eat together so much.

So that night I ate cold pizza while standing at the kitchen counter—this was in March, remember, when we still had a kitchen—and Mom ate yogurt and granola while curled up on the sofa talking to John. She was wearing jeans and a black pullover made out of some nice yarn that might even have been cashmere. She had on lipstick and gold earrings even though she wasn't going anywhere. She was barefoot, and her toenails were red.

Something John said made her laugh, and I thought she looked good—as good as someone who is almost forty ever looks, I mean. Maybe it was because she was finally happy. All the time we were so broke and she was working so hard as a student and then as a peon in the library, she frowned a lot, like a frown was her default expression. Even if you're pretty, you look bad when you're frowning. But now with the new job and Very-Nice Construction and cashmere sweaters, she was smiling.

The sofa sits against the picture window at the front of the house. Beyond Mom, I saw a car pull up to the curb. Elliot.

I waved to get Mom's attention, then mouthed, "Bye!"

She knew I was going out, but I had kind of never gotten around to telling her there was an actual boy involved.

Mom told John to hang on. "Wait a minute, sweetie. Where is it you're going?"

"Uh . . . Tivoli?"

"Tivoli?" she said. "In Belletoona? Is it a special occasion? Since when do you girls hang out there?"

"Yeah, I know, Mom," I said. "Crazy. Bye."

Mom said, "Slow down, Jane. Is Stacy driving? It's a school night. What time will you be home?"

"Oh, you know, Mom. Not late."

She raised her eyebrows. "When's 'not late'?"

"By ten's not late," I said. "Okay? I've got my cell phone. Love you."

Mom put the receiver back to her ear. I moved fast toward the front door—but not fast enough. "Honey?" Mom stopped me. "One other thing."

Would I never get out of here? *"What?"*

Mom smiled. "John says tell you to have fun."

Chapter Twelve

Reason Twelve: Because no matter how polite boys act at first, there's bound to be trouble later.

Trying to escape my mom's questions—and John's helpful advice—I flew out of the house so fast, I almost collided with Elliot on his way up the walk.

All the magazine articles I ever read about romance say a girl should never look too eager. And here was Jane throwing herself into the boy's arms.

"Hey, guess you're really looking forward to dessert, huh?" Elliot said.

Thank goodness it was dark already. Otherwise it would have been, see Jane blush.

"Oh, gosh, hi. Yeah, well, I—I do—uh—like dessert," I stammered as we headed for his car.

He was wearing khakis and a striped, button-down shirt, which was exactly perfect, I thought—not sweats and a T-shirt, but not church-on-Easter, either. Amy once threatened to break up with a guy—even though he looked like a Benetton model—because he never wore anything but sweatpants. Stacy and I totally supported her in that.

Elliot opened the passenger door for me, and I slid inside. The car was a Honda Accord, obviously his mom's, but it didn't matter. There was something thrilling and new about going in a car with a boy at all—especially one so good-looking, he honestly gave me gooseflesh. I mean, in a car you can't help but be superaware of the person next to you. I had already figured out Elliot didn't smell like cigarettes. That night, cocooned close to him—recycling the same air—I realized he didn't use sweet-smelling chemical products like body spray or mousse, either. He just smelled like boy with an edge of soap, and on Elliot, boy with soap smelled delicious.

We drove east down Irving and turned north onto College, heading toward the new highway that goes to Belletoona. He told me more about fencing; his coach, who is Russian and has a long Russian name I still can't spell; the other guys in his club. He fences with sabers, and each game—they're called bouts—goes fast because you get points for attacking a lot, for being aggressive. He has to wear this vest thing called a lame, which is electronic and registers the score every time it's touched by a blade.

"Does it look like chain mail?" I asked.

He looked away from the road and down at me. Meeting his eyes in that cozy space, I felt a total hair-to-toenails rush. I know this sounds hokey, but it happens to be true that I had never felt that before, not even the time we went to the Bomb-Sniffing Dogs concert in Pittsburgh and I got to see Scissors—he's the bass player and my major crush—live and only fifty feet away.

"What's chain mail?" Elliot asked.

"Like what knights wore if they weren't wearing armor. King Arthur, *Monty Python and the Holy Grail,* you know."

Elliot looked back at the road. "Fencing isn't like that anymore," he said. "It's a totally modern sport now."

I smiled because he said this so seriously, but I bit back my laugh because I could already see fencing was not a topic you joked about with Elliot.

It's a fifteen-minute ride from College Springs to Belletoona, which is small and old and nothing-happening except for Tivoli, a Frosty, a good breakfast place called The Pancake Shop, and a bowling alley.

Tivoli is by the river, just west of the central square. It used to be a flour mill back in the day, but it's been a restaurant as long as I can remember. It's pretty inside—kind of sophisticated. Paintings by local artists hang on the brick walls. Tiny white lights outline the doors and windows. On the tables are candles. It's the kind of place you usually go for dinner on your birthday or for graduation, but you can get just dessert in the café, and it's not that expensive. I didn't know if Elliot was paying or not. I had money just in case.

Elliot held the door for me when we walked in. A hostess with curly hair said hi and led us to the second floor. She was wearing tight black jeans, and I wondered if Elliot was watching her wiggle as she climbed the stairs. Did he think she was pretty? Prettier than me?

The hostess pulled a chair out for me, and Elliot and I sat down. We looked at each other. He smiled.

It had been pretty easy to talk when we were in the car or walking—when we weren't looking right at each other. But now we were face-to-face in a romantic restaurant, and I looked pretty, and he looked handsome, and there was tasteful piano music coming from the speakers and a flickering candle between us—and I panicked.

The skin-tingling rush had passed, and there I was, worrying that somebody had better say something quick because if they didn't, my first-ever date would soon turn *awkward* and *embarrassing.*

I smiled back.

Then the waitress saved us by bringing menus, which gave us each a place to aim our eyes. I know the Tivoli dessert menu down to the punctuation, but I read it anyway. I was so busy reading it, and worrying that by now I should have thought of something fascinating to say, that I jumped when Elliot asked me, "What are you having, Jane?"

"*What?* Sorry."

"You know, dessert?"

"Right," I said. "Chocolate espresso mousse cake. It's my favorite. What are you having?"

"Strawberry tart," he said. "I'm allergic to chocolate."

"You're kidding," I said. "That's *awful.*"

And I meant it, too. For a second I even wondered if I could possibly love a person who didn't eat chocolate. But then I realized maybe it was good—like maybe if we were ever served dessert at a fancy dinner party, I would get to eat his, too, and a second later I had concocted this whole fantasy in which I was dining at the White House (because I had finally become whatever special thing I'm going to become) and Elliot was my date. Dessert was chocolate espresso mousse cake. I ate all of mine and then, very discreetly, switched plates and ate Elliot's.

The president, of course, would notice because you don't get to be president unless you're a keen observer. He would say, "My goodness, Jane, how is it that a girl with such a healthy appetite stays so slender and all-around terrific looking?"

And I would say, "Mr. President, I cannot tell a lie. It's all that marathon running I do. I took it up in high school, you know."

That last part is almost true. I do intend to take up running any day now. But I don't have the right shoes yet.

Meanwhile, back in my actual life, Elliot was telling me about his chocolate allergy, the symptoms.

He said, "All over my body—really itchy, really puffy, all oozy and everything."

I tried to sound sympathetic: "That's terrible. I like chocolate."

Elliot said, "Yeah, most people do," and now we were dangerously close either to exhausting the subject or to an even more detailed description of his allergic reaction, so up against the wall, Jane, soon to be voted Miss Conversational Washout of the Twenty-first Century, said, "Tell me more about fencing. When did you start?"

He started when he was eight because a friend was taking lessons.

Besides saber, you can compete in épée and foil.

Besides the lame, you have to wear a special uniform to protect you, and it's hot—and expensive, as are the special shoes.

Elliot is saving up for a new uniform.

"When you're fencing," I asked, "do you ever think of yourself as somebody in a movie or an old book? Like d'Artagnan? Do you feel like you're dueling for a fair maiden?"

Elliot said, "Fencing is all about focus, Jane. There's no way I think about anything except scoring points and keeping the other guy from scoring off me."

I smiled and nodded, but really I was disappointed. I had been half concocting another fantasy, this one featuring me as an achingly lovely Guinevere, and Elliot—with or without chain mail—as an equally dashing Lancelot. Elliot's answer toasted that fantasy fast.

Still, chocolate espresso mousse cake was excellent consolation. I remember Amy telling me she used to be too self-conscious to eat when she went out with a guy the first time. I learned at Tivoli with Elliot that I do not have this particular problem. When the last crumb was gone, I looked up, and Elliot was smiling at me.

My heart bumped. My cheeks felt prickly. My pulse raced. Elliot reached over and put his hand on top of mine, and I thought, If this is a heart attack, let it be fatal because I will die happy.

Elliot said, "What time do you have to be at school?"

That seemed like a strange question till I remembered Zeta has a flex schedule. I told him 8:10, and he said, "Do you want to take a walk or something? It's only nine."

I said, "Sure," and I wondered if he could see my heart pounding underneath the embroidered daisies on my T-shirt.

Elliot paid the check. I tried to argue, but he said he

invited me, and so that was fair. Then he said, "You can pay next time," which meant he wanted there to be a next time.

This romance stuff seemed pretty good.

The night was cloudy, no stars and no moon, but warm for March. We turned left from Tivoli and walked along the river, flowing shiny black and silent below us. Of course, I had felt weak in the knees before, but till that night I never felt weak in the entire body. I was eager for whatever was going to happen next and also afraid of it.

Then Elliot stopped, and I stopped, too. There was nothing out here but us and the river. This was it. At last. The kiss.

Chapter Thirteen

Reason Thirteen: Because if you hand over your lips, the next thing you know, boys will claim some arbitrary, unrelated body part you're not necessarily ready to give up quite yet.

Since I was about nine, I have studied movie kisses in the unlikely event that someday somebody might actually want to kiss me. From studying, I knew pretty much how kisses are supposed to go: The guy and the girl look intently at each other for two to five seconds, then one or the other—usually the guy—leans forward a fraction of an inch, and the other other, usually the girl, responds by closing her eyes and leaning forward, too. Now the guy closes his eyes, and things speed up. Both guy and girl lean like crazy, at the same time twisting their faces in opposite directions to avoid the dreaded nose-collision. Closer . . . closer . . . and—contact. They lock lips.

Once lip-lock has been achieved, a number of variations are possible. In G-rated movies and on the Disney Channel—like say it's parents doing the kissing—everybody's lips remain shut tight and the actual contact portion of the kiss lasts about one second. At the other extreme in the sexy movie you sneaked into because your mom told you you absolutely weren't allowed to see it till you were twenty-five and safely married, there's the kiss where everybody's jaws gape like they're auditioning for a dental school video.

We were there on the walk in the dark, and Elliot said, "Jane, I think you are really cute." Then he leaned toward me, and that's when years of study paid off because I knew to pick up my cue and lean toward him. He closed his eyes and twisted his head to avoid nose-collision. I closed my eyes and twisted my head, too.

So far so good. I felt Elliot's breath on my face, and it was a lovely, strawberry-scented feeling. But now came the tricky part—his lips homing in on mine while somehow at the same time mine homed in on . . . his nose. That's right. I kissed the side of his nose—more accurately, his right nostril.

At least I didn't lick it.

He said, "Oh, sorry."

And I said, "I'm not very good at this."

But my mouth was smashed against his face, which made conversation difficult.

There was some general, slightly soggy face mashing, which did not in any way seem cinematic to me, and then, finally, through a series of maneuvers that might have been pleasant if I had felt less like a dork, our lips—all four of them—found each other.

Yes! We were kissing! Lips and tongues and the occasional clicking of teeth!

At first, it was not a total success. I was, for example, worried the chocolate residue in my mouth might trigger his hives.

But then, pretty quickly, it got better . . . and better. Nice sensations shot through me as I felt his warmth, his strength, how unlike a girl—or a relative—he was. In fact, I had entirely stopped thinking about the story I'd tell Amy and

Stacy, or Elliot's hives, or anything at all except how happy I was, how good this all felt—when complications set in.

What was going on with his hands, anyway? He only had two the last time I counted, but all of a sudden, they seemed to be everywhere.

Not wanting to stop the proceedings entirely, I pushed away gently, like I wanted air, and said, "Hey, Elliot." At the same time, I moved one of his hands a few ribs lower on my rib cage.

Elliot, stronger than me, slid the hand back again, saying all innocent, "What? Oh, Janie. Come on. It's just that you're so *cute*." He was chewing on my ear between words, and there were these little air currents going into my ear, and I surrendered again—till his other hand had slid under my T-shirt and began fiddling unsuccessfully with the clasp of my bra.

"*Elliot*." I pushed back and smiled, apologetic, and looked into his face, which was flushed, and his eyes, which were shiny—sort of like a kid's contemplating a lollipop.

He said, "Come on, Janie. Don't be like that. I *like* you, okay? Hey, I have an idea. How 'bout if we go back to the car?"

I said, "I need to get home. It's a school night, remember? I mean, my mom will be wondering . . ."

Elliot said, "What could be more romantic, Jane? A warm night? A sweet dessert? The river? You?"

I tried to make a joke about his mom's car, the steering wheel, the gearshift—but he answered, "So we go in the backseat," which was not what I was suggesting.

We were walking back toward the Tivoli parking lot now. I felt awful—so awful I decided to talk myself into giving in. Why not? What did it matter if he got his hands under my bra? He was way good-looking. Polite. He had bought me dessert. He was perfect, right? The boy I had been waiting for?

I remembered the way I felt about him after he rescued Tiffany, the way I felt just now at the table when he took my hand. And wasn't kissing him as wonderful as I had hoped it would be?

But I couldn't talk myself into it. I wasn't ready for anything besides kissing. I mean, I'm not some prude. I know plenty of girls wouldn't think twice, and that's fine for them—but it wasn't fine for me. Not that night.

"Backseat?" he said hopefully when we got back to the car.

"I need to get home."

Elliot shrugged, and walked around to the driver's side without opening my door. We drove in silence for maybe ten minutes. Finally I said, "You're mad."

Jane the So-Insightful.

Elliot steered the car off the highway and onto College Drive. Now we were only about a block from my house. Finally, he shook his head the way a dog shakes off a bath, and said, "No, it's okay." Then he looked down at me, and his face wasn't flushed anymore; it was normal again—normal and really, really attractive. I felt like an idiot and a coward.

Elliot said, "I just didn't realize that you were so inexperienced."

Chapter Fourteen

Reason Fourteen: Because a lot of the time boys make you feel like an idiot.

Here is how the first real date of my life ended that night in March.

Elliot walked me halfway up the walk, put his hands on my shoulders, and kissed me on the forehead, which made me feel exactly like a four-year-old. Then he turned away, and I felt this monster bubble rise inside me: regret, sadness, humiliation.

So I dropped to my knees, and I cried out to him: "Stop, Elliot! Come back! Lay me down in the backseat! Tear my almost new daisy T-shirt to shreds if you want to! Only, please, *please* don't go!"

Okay, I didn't really.

Instead, in my usual articulate Jane-fashion and still on my own two feet, I called out, "Hey?"

And Elliot, equally articulate, said, "Yeah?"

And I said, "See you at work?"

And he said, "Yeah, sure, whatever," which, you can imagine, did not improve matters any.

I felt pretty much numb when I walked into the house a few seconds later. Mom was on the sofa reading. I might've thought she never moved since earlier, only she was wearing her flannel pajamas with pictures of books on them, so she must at least have gone upstairs to change.

"Hey, sweetie, did you have fun?" she asked.

Stupidly, I hesitated like it was a difficult question—because it *was* a difficult question.

"Are you okay?" Mom asked. "Who was that boy, anyway?"

Oh, shoot. Busted.

"I can't believe John told you!" I said.

Mom looked honestly puzzled. "Who told me?" she asked.

"John didn't tell you?"

"John? What are you talking about? I know you were out with a boy because I looked out the window!"

"Oh." I was in no mood to talk to my mom about my evening. I wanted to stomp upstairs and enjoy being miserable all on my own. But being mysterious or starting a fight would only lead to another set of problems. "That boy's name is Elliot," I said. "I know him from Seymour's."

"Good-looking," she said, "from what I could see. Was it just the two of you?"

I nodded.

"Hmm," she said. "Is it . . . um . . . a boyfriend kind of thing?"

"No," I said. "I don't know. You're not going to ask a lot of questions, are you?"

"You look a little—I don't know—shell-shocked? You're sure you're all right?" she asked.

Oh, Mom, I thought. I wish I could sit down on the edge of the sofa and tell you everything, and that would make it better—like when I was little. At the same time, I wish I could run for it. I compromised—stayed standing but kept talking, told her where we went, what we ate, that Elliot fences.

"Interesting," Mom said. "But be careful, Jane."

"Be careful?" I repeated.

"You realize at your age there are a lot of things more important than boys. Like grades, for example. And it's particularly important for a girl to be independent because—"

Not this again. I interrupted her. "You're *not* going to spazz out on me, are you? Like you did when I brought home Josh Silberman's Star of David necklace?"

"Josh who?"

"You know, Mom. The time in first grade when that kid asked me to marry him."

Mom shook her head. "Honey, I don't even remember if I ate lunch today; I certainly don't remember any marriage proposals you received in first grade."

"Yes, you do," I said.

My mom let the book fall into her lap and held up her palms in the gesture that means, I'm hopeless; I know it; I'm sorry, and that's what convinced me she really *didn't* remember, which was so strange. All my life that event had been so important to me—that Josh had given me the necklace, that my mom wouldn't let me keep it, that it was her fault my one and only romance had lasted less than a day. Finding out now that she didn't remember was like finding out it had never happened.

Jane Undergoes Identity Quake.

I sat down on the sofa. I tried to explain about Josh Silberman. I didn't do the greatest job, but Mom seemed to get it, sort of.

"So you're saying you think I'm anti-male?" she said.

"Well, yeah, I guess. I mean, you don't even like Bruce!"

"I do, too!" Mom said. "I only wish—"

"They'd get married. I know, Mom."

Mom smiled. "So okay, I guess maybe I was a little anti-male once upon a time, Jane. Your dad's . . . *behavior*," she said carefully, "hurt a lot. It made me gun-shy, if that makes sense to you. But time passes, and things change."

I could have pointed out that some things don't change. I mean, she had barely gone out with a man in the thirteen years since my dad left. She always claimed she was too busy for another relationship. True, a couple of times lately—since she got the fancy new job—she had gone to faculty deals with the president of the university. His name's Brendan Bond, and he's divorced, too. But that was mostly just for work, Mom said, not personal.

Anyway, by then it was late, and I was tired, and I didn't see how I could process the whole thing with Elliot, let alone some big discussion with my mom about *men*.

So I just said, "I think I'll go to bed."

And she yawned and said she was right behind me.

Before going upstairs, I went to the kitchen for water. On the counter I remember there were teacups—two teacups, with saucers. Since when did we even use teacups, let alone saucers? We use mugs for everything. Had they been there

71

earlier? Had Mom had some kind of company-worth-a-teacup while I was with Elliot?

I was going to ask her, but when I came out of the kitchen, she had already gone to bed.

Upstairs, I brushed my teeth, threw my clothes on the floor, and pulled a size XL T-shirt over my head. While I did this, I kept my mind absolutely blank. It is possible to do this if you concentrate. It is sort of like holding your breath. The second I was in bed, though, my thoughts came in a flood:

Was I a loser? Or was Elliot a jerk?

Or neither? Or both?

For years Stacy and Amy had been my primo sources of information on boy behavior. From them I had learned about boys who try to pull your jeans off the first time they got you alone, boys who beg you to pull their jeans off, and boys who require a permission slip before they hold your hand.

But personal experience? Well, you already know all there is to know about Josh Silberman.

As I lay there a terrible thought occurred to me. Was I *like* my mom? *Worse* than my mom?

Amy and Stacy had always said I was waiting for Mr. Perfect, but maybe I was waiting because I was scared. Maybe I was gun-shy, the way my mom said she was—only I had never even been in battle.

Chapter Fifteen

Reason Fifteen: Because crying scares away the customers.

Today is Thursday, August 10. Elliot and I have been broken up for two weeks and one day. But who's counting?

I'm at work. It's right after the morning rush. Seymour calls me into his office. This has never happened before, but I don't have time to worry about it. When Loren tells me Seymour wants to see me, I just wipe the mayo off and go.

Seymour is standing behind his big desk. He is short, round, and mostly bald. He is about—I am guessing—sixty years old. Seymour has never been married, which is too bad because he looks like he really ought to be somebody's grandpa.

I sit down. Seymour looks at me and recites from the employee manual: "Laugh and the world buys bagels, cry and you drive the customers out the door."

I know right away what he means. Twice since the whole mess with Elliot, I have started to cry here at work. Everybody was really nice about it, but it's true—we haven't been very busy lately. I thought it was probably Panacho being open, but maybe it's me? And now Seymour is firing me.

Naturally, I start to cry. "Okay," I say. "I'll go."

Seymour gets flustered, yanks a tissue out of the box on his desk, and hands it to me. "No, Jane—*no*. You misunderstand. I was only thinking perhaps you might want to do something other than working out front? Something where your grim countenance won't interfere with sales?"

"Are you saying I'm scary?" I ask.

Seymour smiles. "You are one of my best employees, Jane. I don't want to lose you just because you've been through difficulties of the heart. So what about this? What if you try your hand at developing a theme for our float in the Kickoff Parade?"

I'm so surprised, I blurt what's in my head instead of thinking first. "But there's only sixteen days left! We all figured it was too late!"

Seymour sighs. "It's true I haven't been able to concentrate on the parade, or much of anything else lately," he says. "I don't mind telling you I'm pretty worried about . . ." He drops his voice in case any Panacho spies are around. "About the competition."

"I know," I say.

But then he rallies. "It's never too late, though, Jane— never too late for a fine bagel, as it says in the employee handbook. Andrea will do the drawings as usual, but she thought—we both thought—a new perspective on the theme might be in order."

Seymour reaches into the supply closet, then comes around the desk and hands me a yellow legal pad, a sharp pencil, and the rest of the box of Kleenex.

"Make yourself comfortable," he says, and he waves toward his chair.

"I get to use your desk?"

"Yes, you do," he says. "And I will take your shift. I only hope I remember how to make a lunch special."

Here's how small College Springs is: The Kickoff Parade is, like, the big deal of the year. Everybody for miles around is either in it or watching it. Besides the floats, there are fire engines; Girl Scouts and Boy Scouts; horses; clowns; herds of small, uncoordinated, and frequently dangerous baton twirlers; and marching bands from all over the state—the kids dragged home from their summer vacations to rehearse.

I want to do a good job, so I start by thinking about other floats I've seen. The one Andrea designed last year was the best. It looked like the *Queen Mary II*. Sharks "swam" next to it, and every few minutes a well-dressed passenger tipped out of a deck chair and fell in with a splash that came from an ornamental fountain borrowed from a nursery. After that, all the peons playing passengers ran around on deck, and the sharks schooled, and then—right before the victim's certain death in a crush of cruel, serrated jaws—the captain of the ship, Seymour himself, tossed a life preserver and saved the day.

The life preserver was really an oversized egg bagel with SEYMOUR'S stenciled on it in poppy seeds. Kids loved it. And sales of egg bagels were off the chart right through Labor Day.

I think it will be a relief to think about something besides whether Elliot is actually going out with Valerie or with anybody, whether I hate him, whether he hates me, whether I am going to live the rest of my life as a single woman, whether there possibly could be anything worse than being without him.

But after I've sat at Seymour's desk for two hours, all I have is a list of bad ideas:

- Bagels that leap tall buildings in a single bound
- Satellite bagels from outer space
- Fairy-tale princesses wearing bagel crowns
- Cops and robbers with bagel handcuffs
- Angels with bagel halos
- Bagels that tap-dance

I am about to give up, find Seymour, tell him to send me back to pastrami and pickles for good, when the door opens and Arthur appears.

"So? How flow the creative juices?" he asks me.

There is something about Arthur I didn't mention before. He often wears skirts. I don't mean necessarily that he's gay. I'm not sure in that department *what* he is. I like to think he wears skirts mostly because they are the best expression of his keenly developed fashion sense. He himself says it's because of his unique need to be very very *Arthur.*

Anyway, today he is wearing a green Seymour's shirt with a particularly elegant skirt, one I haven't seen before, white tulle with a pattern of gold stars.

"Stylish," I say.

"You like it?" Arthur tugs a ruffle. "It was a prom dress, I think. I cut off the bottom and added a waistband."

"The stars remind me of magic wands—like the Good Witch of the North," I say.

"I thought badges—a sheriff in the Old West," Arthur says.

"Wearing the bottom half of a prom dress?" I say.

"True," Arthur says. "It ought to be gingham. Grace Kelly in *High Noon*."

And that's when *pow*—the lightning strikes at last. "Wait a second," I say. "*That is it!* Isn't it? Duel on Main Street! The sheriff and the outlaw! Featuring Seymour as . . . *the sheriff*!"

I jot down some notes and five minutes later explain my concept to Seymour. I am excited. "Can't you just see it? The float depicts a small western town—pinto ponies . . . uh . . . hitching posts for pinto ponies, saloons . . . uh . . . snow-capped peaks, poker, you know . . . townsfolk, stagecoaches, a railroad depot . . . pinto ponies—"

Seymour nods. "I get it. Jane. Ponies."

"Right! And right in the middle of the hot, dusty main street—*you*!"

"Me?"

"You! Dressed up as the sheriff—get it? White hat. Gold star. . . ."

Seymour looks thoughtful. "I've always wanted cowboy boots."

I nod. "You can have them, too, Seymour. You're the boss!"

"So the concept is . . . ?"

"This town ain't big enough for the both of us!" I say. "And Seymour's are the good-guy bagels, the bagels that represent truth and justice, the bagels that represent mom and apple pie, Grace Kelly and Gary Cooper, the bagels from your hometown!"

Seymour likes it. I can tell. But there is one more person to convince, and I am afraid she might not be so agreeable. In my experience Witch Lady has never been agreeable about anything. Plus, was it really okay with her that I come up with the theme this year? Isn't that her job? Somebody told me once she went to art school back in the day. But if that's true, why is she managing a bagel store?

Anyway, Seymour goes to talk to her in her office. When he comes back, he is smiling. "She's delighted, Jane," he says. "She'll start drawing right away. You know, she and I go back a dozen years, and when I told her your idea . . . well, it was the first time I ever heard her laugh."

Chapter Sixteen

*Reason Sixteen: Because even a boy with
a good butt may have bad taste.*

I met Arthur the first day I went to work at Seymour's. That
was March, right after my sixteenth birthday.

Loren was the one assigned to train me for my job, my first
paying job. Loren is small and wiry, with freckles. That day she
was dressed in tight jeans and her Seymour's T-shirt, with a
pink bandanna in her red hair. I felt big and sweaty next to her.

Right away, the two of us had this confusion about my
name.

Loren said, "Come on. Shoot. I'm sorry. I forgot already.
What's your name again? Jane, right?"

I said, "Jane, yeah."

She said, "Janeya—I like it. Janeya sounds like Russian or
something. There was a Russian girl in my gym class. She had
like these really big thighs and no boobs. Guys liked her, some
guys, which was surprising because no boobs, right?"

"Actually," I said, "it isn't Janeya. My name. It's only Jane."

"Only Jane?" she said.

I felt bad for a minute, like my ordinariness disappointed
her, and I said I was sorry, but my name was on my birth certificate and I didn't think I could do anything about it at least till I

was eighteen. She started showing me behind the sandwich counter, mustard and mayonnaise and vinegar and Robbie, who was slapping slices of turkey onto a whole wheat bagel.

Recognizing that the bagel was whole wheat gave me a flash of confidence, and I thought maybe it would turn out I had a talent for bagels. Maybe I would own Seymour's one day. I would change the name to Janeya's. I would add papaya smoothies to the menu, and ice-cream sodas, and lemon cake like Grandma makes for Easter. I would put rhinestones on the T-shirts and replace the bandannas with Panama hats. The peons would worship me. Bagels would be my life.

Robbie nodded, but did not say hi. He squeezed mayonnaise from a plastic bottle onto the turkey. Seeing the mayonnaise like that—so much of it—my stomach did a little hiccup, and I quickly reconsidered. Maybe bagels would not be my life. Maybe every shift I worked I would spend in the bathroom puking.

Loren said, "The hard part is dealing with the customers, all their questions. Like it's a football weekend, and there are one hundred and seventy people in line and you get a customer who can't decide what he wants, so he asks you, 'What does provolone taste like?' And what are you supposed to say? Sweaty socks? I mean, because to me personally, all cheese tastes like sweaty socks."

I didn't answer, because I like cheese, but I was afraid Loren would think I was rude if I said so. My food issues are all about avocados, which are slimy and taste like the green stuff that grows on the inside of a goldfish bowl if you forget to change the water. I hoped no customer ever asked me about avocados.

80

After Loren introduced me to Robbie, she took me over to where the cash register was, and that's where Arthur was working. So this was the first time I ever saw Arthur, who was destined to become my best work friend. Arthur has pale skin and big brown eyes—sort of like a character out of manga, except taller. Arthur did not have any customers to ring up right then, so he was leaning his long, skinny self on the horseshoe counter that surrounds the cash register and reading the label on a tub of coffee creamer.

Arthur said, "What do you suppose that polysorbate 60 does to your body?" and Loren said, like this explained anything, "Arthur wants to be a costume designer on Broadway someday," and I said, "Polysorbate 60 is an emulsifier."

Arthur raised his eyebrows.

I said, "It's in the creamer junk so the oil won't separate out from whatever else is in the creamer junk. It's fine to your body. You can look it up."

Loren said, "Wow," but Arthur was not impressed, and I wondered if maybe he was that kind of person, the kind where fate always sent him the answer to his questions.

Arthur said, "Let us consider high fructose corn sweetener." He had picked up a packet of ketchup. I would have told him that from the point of view of your body, it's no different than sugar, but a person ought to watch his sugar consumption in general because so many processed foods are loaded with it, and it only adds calories, not nutrition.

Which I learned from a carton of my mom's soy milk.

Like I said, I would have told him that, but at that moment the guy with the turkey on whole wheat came up to pay.

Arthur smiled exactly the way the employee handbook says to, and then said, "Will there be anything else today, sir?"

The man shook his head.

Arthur punched the register. "That will be five-oh-nine and the title of your favorite movie."

The man was confused. He handed Arthur money and said, "What else was it you wanted?"

Arthur said, "Your favorite movie, sir."

The man said, "Why?"

Loren whispered to me, "Sometimes he asks song."

Without answering, the man took his change and his sandwich and headed for a faraway table, like he was scared Arthur might come after him with more questions.

Arthur watched him go, then turned to me and said, "Are you easily threatened?" He was about to say something else, but Witch Lady's voice came from her office: "Arthur! We need more cream cheese up here."

Arthur looked at me, then he looked at Loren, then he made a tragic face and said, "I guess this is good-bye." He came out from behind the horseshoe counter. He was wearing the usual Seymour's T-shirt. His bandanna was jade green, which was a good match for his sarong, which was a cotton wraparound like the ones Hawaiian guys wear. In New York City I wouldn't have blinked at a guy wearing a floral-print sarong, but here in College Springs?

Loren acted like this was nothing unusual, though, so what was I supposed to do? I acted like this was nothing unusual, too.

Chapter Seventeen

Reason Seventeen: Because not kissing boys leaves you with a lot of free time you can spend doing other, more worthwhile, un-boy-related type things.

(Friday, August 11, two weeks and two days A.E., After Elliot. Stacy, Amy, and I are sitting at a window table at Seymour's. Stacy has two cinnamon rolls. I have a blueberry muffin. Amy is dunking a tea bag in hot water.)

ME: I knew you'd make it, Amy! First chair!

AMY: It just means more rehearsal and more practice. I am like a *victim* of clarinet.

STACY: Clarinet and Sunday school and the equestrian center—and what about Tony?

AMY: He made all-state, too, which is good because otherwise I'd never see him.

ME: What's he play again?

AMY: Don't laugh. Bassoon.

(Stacy and I laugh.)

STACY: There is something sexy about a man who plays bassoon, I mean, when you think about it.

AMY: Cut it out, Stacy.

STACY: No, really. I mean, any boy can play piccolo or trumpet or tuba, but it takes a *man* to play—

ME: Leave her alone, Stacy.

STACY: I was just being supportive, like always. Where does he go to school again?

AMY: Golden Eagle.

ME: Do they march in the Kickoff Parade?

AMY: Not this year, unfortunately. I won't see him that weekend, either. But hey, Jane, what's up with your float? Do you need us to help with the build?

ME *(looks around, lowers voice):* You remember it's all secret, right? You can't tell what I told you yesterday about the theme and all?

STACY: Of course we know it's secret.

AMY: It's not like we don't know the rules or something.

ME: Okay, well, Witch Lady—I mean, *Andrea*—got the drawings done already. They are *so great*. I never knew she drew like that.

STACY: Well, *yeah*! She had like a full scholarship to University of the Arts.

ME: Oh, is it you that told me about her? I can't remember how come you even know her.

STACY: They're our neighbors down the street—used to be. She was my sisters' baby-sitter. Then she went away to school; then she had to come back because her mom got totally sick; then her dad got totally sick. In the end she quit school to take care of them.

AMY: Oh, gosh, that's sad.

STACY: Really sad. It's not like they were even that old or anything. Finally, I guess her mom died, and her dad had to go into a convalescent place.

AMY: So now she can go back to art school.

STACY: Now she's too old for art school.

AMY: Maybe she likes working in a bagel store.

STACY: Who would like working in a bagel store? Oh, sorry, Jane.

ME: It's okay. I'm not a really talented artist or anything like Andrea is.

AMY: You have to stop being so hard on yourself. You're good at a lot of things—like school, and . . . uh . . . interpersonal relationships.

ME: Interpersonal relationships?

STACY: She means being friends with us. But you're not so good at interpersonal relationships with boys.

AMY: No.

STACY: The trouble is, Jane, you don't *understand* boys. You haven't had enough experience. You need like a class or something to catch you up. I mean, you're good at school, so a class is the logical thing.

ME: And who's going to teach that class?

STACY: Dr. Stacy!

ME: I kind of had a feeling. . . .

STACY: Lesson One: Going out with guys is a big game— never take it seriously.

AMY *(dips tea bag, nods sincerely)*.

ME *(looks at each in turn):* I can't believe you two! You are total, total liars. Stace was a basket case for a month after Kevin broke up with her—you *were*! And Amy's been like floating on air since she met Tony, sexy bassoon player, at band camp.

AMY: Would you give me a break on the bassoon thing?

STACY: In fact, here is Lesson Two: It's better not even to go out with boys.

AMY: It is?

STACY: Because think of all the time it gives you, Jane! Time for making moola! Time for shopping! Time for school, and girlfriends, and being the number one fan of Bomb-Sniffing Dogs!

AMY: Lesson Two is not very helpful, Stace.

STACY: Lesson Three: Take care never to damage a boy's delicate masculine pride.

AMY *(nods):* They hate it if you do that.

ME: What are you talking about—"delicate masculine pride"?

STACY: That's what you did to Elliot, Jane. You told him your mom grounded you at work that day, right? Right before he grabbed Valerie?

ME: Right.

STACY: Well, he thought you were using your mom as an excuse to reject him—especially after what happened at my house and all. He saw that as rejection big-time. He was wounded!

AMY: Yeah—like in the jungle. A wounded predator. Guys get that way. Stacy and I figured this out on the phone last night.

ME: You were talking about Elliot and me on the phone last night?

STACY: Oh, like this is some big surprise. What else would we be talking about?

AMY: So with Elliot, it was like whatchamacallit, insult to injury. After what happened at Stacy's party—

ME: Let's not talk about that.

AMY *(waves her hands)*: Okay, okay. Only there's nothing wrong with what you did.

ME: Only that afterward Elliot broke up with me.

STACY: The timing was bad.

AMY: Besides, if you think about it, it wasn't *bad* luck at all. You should be *glad* to be done with him. So it was *good* luck!

STACY: That would be Lesson Four. You should be taking notes.

AMY: You want to know what the main problem with guys is?

STACY: Lesson Five.

AMY: Most of them waste their brain cells on non-essentials, crap like sports stats and entire monologues from comedians on TV.

STACY: The plots of cartoons.

AMY: Cars. Video games.

STACY: Oh, yeah. Video games, definitely.

ME *(shaking my head emphatically)*: Not all guys! Arthur isn't like that! And for that matter, what about Ashok?

STACY: And do you want to go *out* with Arthur or Ashok?

ME: Of course not. But Tony—what about Tony? And even Elliot wasn't *that* bad.

STACY: What did you talk about with Elliot, I mean most of the time?

ME: Most of the time? Uh . . . fencing.

(Stacy and Amy look at each other.)

AMY: And honestly? Even though Tony is mostly perfect, he is a huge Yankees fan.

STACY: Oh, gross! You're kidding!

ME: You wouldn't expect that from a bassoon player.

AMY *(distracted, looking out window):* There's something going on, on the sidewalk. Look, you guys.

ME: Probably Panacho again. You know how they try to steal our customers? They send that dumb guy in a dragon suit down here, and he hands out coupons practically in front of our door!

STACY: You're right—the dragon's out there. But it's some old guy that's attracting the crowd.

ME: Oh, you're right. Hey—weird. It's Mr. Black!

STACY AND AMY: Who?

ME: You know. You've seen him around. I wonder if he's working for Panacho.

AMY: What's that sign he's holding?

STACY: I can't read it. A lot of people are laughing, though, so I guess it's like a joke.

ME *(shakes head):* I don't think so. Mr. Black doesn't exactly have a sense of humor.

STACY: Wait—now he's shouting something. Oh—and he's turned the sign so I can read it: SEYMOUR'S BAGELS ARE A SIN.

Chapter Eighteen

Reason Eighteen: Because when agitated, boys can be dangerous.

Drivers honk their horns. Pedestrians stop and point. Mr. Black smiles and waves to them all like he thinks the people of College Springs are truly grateful for someone with the guts to take a stand against date nut bagels.

The Panacho dragon waves, too, but—I'm happy to say—nobody seems to be paying much attention to him.

A few moments pass, and Mr. Black's expression changes from smile to frown. He has seen something approaching on the sidewalk. Still inside Seymour's, I strain to catch his words: ". . . exactly the kind of decadent display you'd expect where tradition is flouted!" he hollers. "Further evidence of the decline . . ."

The knot of people shifts, and I see what Mr. Black is looking at: It is Arthur, arriving punctually to cover his lunch shift. He is wearing his Seymour's T-shirt and an aquamarine bias-cut skirt with white pinstripes. I can't help thinking it looks a lot better on him than it would on me.

"Hey," says Stacy. "Isn't that your friend Arthur, Jane? And wow—check out that skirt!"

"I don't believe it!" Amy says. "I have looked and *looked* for something to match my new sweater. Does he ever share? I'd dry-clean it, I swear."

"Is he okay out there with the crazy guy?" Stacy has kicked into caregiver mode. "Does he need help?"

I remember the day I didn't help Tiffany with Mr. Black, the day I let Elliot come to the rescue.

I stand up. "Come on," I say.

"This is not the way I pictured my one hour of freedom," Amy says, but she stands up, too, and in a second we are on the sidewalk: three girls on a rescue mission.

Only Arthur does not realize he needs rescue and so far is holding his own: "In the South Seas, in Southeast Asia, in Scotland—"

Mr. Black interrupts: "Who is speaking of pagan cultures? We are right here—"

". . . practical, functional, *and* easy-care—"

". . . fathers, mothers, precious babes—"

". . . *variety* of styles and colors—"

". . . pants for women! Dresses for men!" Mr. Black says firmly, like these will be his last words on the subject—until he realizes he has said the opposite of what he means. He tries to start over, but people are walking away, bored with him. Arthur turns away, too. He is heading inside to work.

But Mr. Black has been enjoying the attention. He doesn't want to give it up. So he makes a bold and dramatic gesture: He bashes Arthur in the head with his sign.

Maybe you wouldn't expect a cardboard sign wielded by a skinny old man to hurt a hard teenage head. But you wouldn't be counting on (a) the heavy wood post the sign was attached to, or (b) the intensity of Mr. Black's opposition to Seymour's bagels, not to mention teenage boys in skirts.

The sign connects with a *thwack*. Poor Arthur stiffens, looks dazed, shuts his eyes, and crumples to the sidewalk.

Cell phones pop from pockets, and *be-be-be-be-beep*, several people dial 9-1-1 at the same time.

"We need an ambulance . . ."

"*Yes*, police! An assault . . ."

"No, no—the *old* guy is fine. It's the young one . . ."

Amy runs into Seymour's: "I'll get some water."

Stacy kneels by Arthur and coos, "Sweetie? Can you talk?"

I pick up Mr. Black's sign, the weapon. Mr. Black is standing back, looking shaky, like flattening sinners isn't as much fun as he expected it to be.

By the time Amy comes back with the water, Arthur has opened his eyes and is leaning on his elbows.

Someone says, "Son, can you stand?" and someone else asks, "How many fingers am I holding up?"

The Panacho dragon is still hovering, trying to give away coupons. Arthur catches sight of it, and his eyes widen. He probably thinks he's hallucinating.

I grab Mr. Black's sign from the sidewalk and wave it at the dragon. *"Shoo!"* I say. "You get out of here!"

Amy says, "*Yeah*, can't you see you're scaring him?"

The dragon hangs its head and skulks away.

"All gone," Stacy says to Arthur.

Arthur nods and rubs his head. "Right." Then he looks into Stacy's face. "Uh . . . do I know you?"

"Stacy," she says. "Jane's friend?"

"The famous Dr. Stacy," he says.

Meanwhile, sirens squeal, and a few moments later an ambulance and a police car pull up to the curb. Out of the police car steps Officer Giuseppe "Joe" Capparella. We all know him because he's the cop who visits schools to tell us not to drink or spray-paint graffiti or do anything else that might give him extra work.

The ambulance brakes with a lurch and then seems to explode—all the doors bursting open and people flying out carrying equipment, including a stretcher.

"Give 'em room," says Officer Capparella, who is calm and slow compared with the ambulance guys.

"What? Jeez, no . . . is all this for . . . ?" Arthur is still woozy but awake enough to be embarrassed.

"Lie back and be quiet," says Officer Capparella. "The knot on your head's pretty good, son. Now"—he looks around—"who would like to tell me what happened here?"

Chapter Nineteen

Reason Nineteen: Because if you consider what men and boys like to eat, it's enough to give you a bellyache.

Arthur does not die. He doesn't even have to go to the hospital. Andrea sends him home to recuperate. Stacy volunteers to drive him. Jennifer picks Amy up for her yoga class. Officer Capparella tells Mr. Black he can leave—for the time being.

"But be somewhere I can find you," Capparella says sternly.

"Where would I go?" Mr. Black says.

Seymour arrives at last—he has been out at the barn where the float will be built. Capparella catches him up with what's happened and asks if they can have a chat in his office. Seymour says sure, would he like a bite of something?

Capparella nods, and Seymour turns to me. "Jane, are you still on the clock?"

"Not technically, Seymour."

"You want to do me a favor, then?"

I smile. "Sure."

"Can you get Officer Capparella his usual?"

I can't help it, I make a face. "An onion bagel and a nonfat caramel latte?"

Capparella smiles.

My stomach hiccups, but I say, "Coming right up."

When I bring the food to Seymour's office, Capparella is talking.

Seymour interrupts. "Stick around a minute, Jane—if you don't mind," he says. "I may need sustenance myself, but I'm not so decisive as our friend here."

I want to listen, so I try to blend into the background. Maybe they'll forget about me.

"Like I'm saying," Capparella goes on. "The guy is a classic narcissistic type—we learned all about 'em at the police academy. Too much mother love, that's the problem. He never got over it, craves constant attention. How'm I doing so far?"

Seymour nods. "Go on, Joe. What are you saying?"

Capparella is in no hurry. "What do you do with a narcissist?" he asks. "Well, if it's a kid, you get 'em on a team or in Boy Scouts—positive peer pressure."

"Herman is hardly a kid," says Seymour.

"Work with me here, Seymour. He's what? Five years older than you are?"

"Right," Seymour says, and I wonder how come Seymour knows that. Did they used to be friends?

"Guy needs to feel he's a part of something greater than he is, an *enterprise* greater than he is," Capparella says. "And he can obviously use a paycheck, maybe some leftover muffins now and again. . . . Are you catching my drift?"

"You want me to give him a job," Seymour says.

Capparella points. "Sharp as ever, Professor."

"You know, it's not as if I haven't tried to help him before," Seymour says. "But he doesn't let me. And he's none too polite in his refusals either. He's proud."

Capparella nods. "Classic narcissist. That's what I'm saying. Anyway, this time I have a feeling he'll let you. This time it's work, not a handout."

"The man thinks my bagels are immoral," Seymour reminds him. "And now I'm going to ask him to sell them?"

"He's likely to reconsider his stance on the jalapeño bagel," Capparella says, "when he realizes his alternative is an assault charge and jail time."

"I take your meaning. But what about Arthur?" Seymour asks. "He's the victim."

"I don't think that's going to be a problem," Capparella says, "not if you'll go along."

"And Arthur's parents?" Seymour says.

Capparella shakes his head, makes the universal sign for crazy. "That poor kid. I doubt they even notice the lump on his head."

I am amazed at how much Capparella seems to know about everybody. He's as good as Grandma. A second later I'm even more amazed.

Seymour and Capparella stand up and shake hands.

Capparella says, "D'ja ever think you'd be offering your no-account brother a job?"

"Stepbrother, if you please. And if it doesn't work out, I'll know whom to blame," Seymour says. "Bear in mind, Officer, I can cut you off caramel lattes for good."

The next day is Saturday. Chocolate sodas at Grandma's. She fills in a few details.

"Seymour and Herman grew up in Pittsburgh. Seymour's

mother died when he was a child—I don't know how old exactly. His father married Herman's mother, so they're step-brothers."

"Herman—Mr. Black—is older," I say.

Grandma nods. "That's right. The two of them never got along is what I hear. I guess Herman didn't want a younger brother, especially such a smart younger brother. As soon as he could, he left home—went to California, I think it was. Worked out there for years but finally came back. Meanwhile, Seymour came here to teach. Well, you know *that* story. Anyhow, your mother says I shouldn't gossip."

This is totally true. Mom says this all the time, but now I don't answer. I take a long drink of soda instead.

Grandma reads my mind and laughs. "I defend my right to gossip!"

I try to think of something good about gossip. Finally, I say, "I guess gossip is entertaining. It makes real-life seem more like a soap opera."

"You've got it backward, Jane. Soap operas are like life—only the people are a little sexed-up to sell the advertising. Do you know where the word *gossip* comes from?"

I shake my head no.

"God's words," Grandma says.

"How do you know that?" I ask.

"You and your mom aren't the only ones who look things up."

I smile, embarrassed. "Don't tease me, Grandma."

"I think I'm allowed," she says, and she reaches across to tug a lock of my hair. Grandma is not much of a hugger. For her this is affectionate. "Anyway, gossip is how a group of people—neighbors, a town, a community—talks to itself. We pass the word on right and wrong, who's behaving and who's not, by telling stories about each other. And of course, there are also fairy tales, myths, the Bible. . . ."

"*People* magazine," I say.

She runs her finger around the inner rim of the glass, then licks it. "Exactly."

"Can I ask something personal?" I say.

"Again?" she says.

"Again," I say. "When you and Frank . . . , when you were pregnant . . . was there a lot of gossip?"

Grandma looks thoughtful. "It was a very different time," she says, "nineteen sixty-seven, the Vietnam War in full swing. Sex and drugs and rock 'n' roll. Hippies and free love . . ."

"So no gossip?" I say.

"*Yes* gossip!" she contradicts me. "Because all *that* was in the big city, a million miles from this place. Oh, my—was there gossip."

My mom keeps a photograph of her and Grandma in her room. Grandma has long, dark hair and earrings almost as big as the jade green butterflies she's wearing right now. Mom's about two years old. She's sitting on my grandma's shoulders and laughing. Grandma's smiling, too, but her smile looks fierce.

"I bet the gossip never bothered you, though, did it?" I say. "You were too tough to mind."

"Never bothered me?" Grandma says. "Honey, I walked

that baby—your mother—back and forth long into the night. She had the colic—we were both bawling."

"Then, you're a hypocrite!" I say. "How come you defend gossip now?"

Grandma shrugs. "I did something most people considered wrong; I took my medicine and lived to tell."

"Lived to gossip, you mean."

She laughs. "Exactly. Besides, I can't see how your knowing that Herman Black used to live in California hurts anybody, least of all Herman Black."

I can't argue with that. "I'm the one that's going to train him," I say. "Monday morning."

"Why do you get the honor?" Grandma asks.

"Seymour knows I'm Arthur's good friend. He figured the other peons would see me trying to get along with Mr. Black, and then they'd try to get along with him, too."

"Do they know he's Seymour's stepbrother?" she asks.

"Witch Lady does—I mean, Andrea. But not anybody else I don't think."

Grandma smiles. "Well, honey, I wish you all good luck—especially considering how cranky and unreasonable old people are."

Chapter Twenty

Reason Twenty: Because the human mouth is like a trip to Hawaii if you're a germ; and if you consider all the spit that passes kisser to kissee in a facefest, at some point your immune system gets worn out, and the nasty germs get their chance, and—bingo—you develop a cold.

On Monday, Mr. Black is ten minutes late for his eight o'clock shift. He does not apologize or make an excuse, and Witch Lady lets it go, which I cannot believe. But then I realize she hasn't been quite as witchlike lately as usual. With Seymour so worried about Panacho, she's been running things more. Maybe she likes that. Or maybe she's just excited about the float.

"Jane, this is Mr. Joe Black and vice versa," Witch Lady says. "We have decided to start you at the pastry counter, Mr. Black. Good luck. We hope you enjoy bringing high-quality bagels and baked goods to the people of College Springs."

Mr. Black is thin all over, but he has a potbelly. He looks a little ridiculous in his Seymour's T-shirt, and I am afraid he might smell bad or be dirty. But I sneak a little sniff, and it's okay, nothing. Then I peek at his fingernails. Clean.

I lead him over to the pastry counter and show him the scones, cookies, buns, and bagels. I tell him the prices and show him the crib sheet behind the counter in case he forgets.

I introduce him to the other peons. I tell him the ten and four rule from the employee handbook. If a customer is ten feet away, you must smile at him. If he is four feet away, you must say hello and ask if he needs help.

Mr. Black nods and tries to smile when I tell him to. His smile is more like a display of teeth, but I am pretty sure it's the best he can do. Seeing this, I am thinking maybe your smile muscles atrophy if you don't use them for a long time.

There aren't any customers right now—I'm afraid Seymour is right, and Panacho *is* cutting into business—so we pack up some orders that are going to be picked up later. Mr. Black doesn't say anything. I search my brain for something to talk about while boxing up cinnamon rolls. Finally I pull an Arthur.

"What's your favorite movie?" I ask.

Mr. Black looks interested for the first time all morning. "You like movies?" he asks.

"Sure," I say.

"*Old* movies?" he asks.

"Sure," I say again.

Now he looks suspicious. "*How* old?" he asks. "Because I know with you kids—you probably think five years ago is old."

This is kind of annoying. "When I say old, I mean *old*," I say. "The library over in Pleasant Haven, where my dad lives, doesn't *have* any new movies. When I see my dad, we usually check one out. So I've probably seen every Marx Brothers movie like six times, and all the old musicals, and Jimmy Stewart . . ."

Mr. Black gets a dreamy expression on his face. "I'll tell ya a little secret," he says.

I am not actually sure I want to hear Mr. Black's secret, but I'm supposed to be nice. "What?"

"I was *in* the movies."

"What do you mean *in* the movies?"

"I mean I was an actor!" he says. "In the movies! In Hollywood!" He's talking pretty loudly now. Is he going to get hysterical? I remember the way he was when he lectured poor Tiffany about the origins of the bagel.

"Okay," I say. "Right. You were an actor."

He seems crushed. "You don't believe me," he says.

"Sure, I believe you. Uh . . . what movie were you in?"

"Oh, lots," he says. "Back in the day."

I can't help it—I'm curious. "Name one," I say.

"*Guys and Dolls*," he says.

I forget I don't believe him. "Get out! *Guys and Dolls* is like my *favorite*! Who did you play?"

"I'm a waiter," he says. "Actually, two waiters—first at Mindy's and then in the Havana scene. They put brown makeup and a mustache on me for the Havana scene so I'd look different."

I turn away from the baked goods and sneeze a big fake sneeze. Then I say—just like Vivian Blaine, who plays Adelaide in *Guys and Dolls*—"'A poy-son could develop a cold.'"

Mr. Black grins. "You really *do* know that movie."

I tell him, "Arthur—the kid you bashed on the head yesterday? He loves old movies. He knows way more about them than I do."

Mr. Black looks thoughtful. "Is it possible I could be wrong about him?"

I shrug. "Well, that kind of depends on why you bashed him in the head, doesn't it? If it's because he's different . . . well, no offense, but you're different, too. Oh—this box of cinnamon rolls is for the College Springs Elementary PTA. Mr. Parakeet is going to pick them up at five. Mark the price on the box with the red marker, and set them aside for him. Have you got that?"

"How much are they?" Mr. Black asks.

"Twelve dollars a dozen with the nonprofit discount," I say. "It's on the crib sheet." I point it out to him again.

Mr. Black stares at the sheet, then he shakes his head. "For a little flour, a little sugar?"

"Open your own bagel store if you don't like it." Arthur himself has come up behind us. "That's how free enterprise is supposed to work." Arthur is wearing a skirt stitched together out of old ties from the Salvation Army.

"You and Arthur have already met," I say.

Nervously, Mr. Black looks up into Arthur's face. Arthur is about a foot taller.

"Hey," Arthur says.

Mr. Black nods. This would be an excellent time for him to apologize. But he doesn't, and I guess that might be too much to hope for. So I say, "It turns out the two of you have something in common."

Chapter Twenty-one

Reason Twenty-one: Because it's not only boys who can't be trusted, it's men, too, and that's what boys grow into, given sunshine, rain, and plenty of . . . compost.

At night when I can't sleep, I stare at the orange and yellow sun that's painted on my ceiling. In the dark the colors are only shadows, but the smile is always there.

My dad painted the sun when I was a baby. It is huge—the rays expand corner to corner and drip down the walls. So far as I know, my dad never attempted another piece of artwork, and according to my mom, this is a mercy. His sun is blobby; its grin is lopsided; the nose isn't finished. I think Dad got bored after the first nostril and skipped ahead to the eyes, which would be totally my dad. Anyway, I don't care; I love that sun. When Very-Nice painted my room last year, I wouldn't let them touch the ceiling. I even made Mitch paint around the orange drips on the wall.

My dad left my mom when I was three. What happened is this: At bedtime one night, my dad didn't come to tuck me in, and he didn't wake me the next morning, either. Instead, there was a phone call.

I think I remember that conversation, but I can't be sure. Actually, since the identity quake over Josh Silberman's Star of David I am trusting my memory less and less. Now I think that sometimes something happens in your life and it turns out to be important, so you think back on it a lot, and it's possible that when you think back on it, you change it. You might do it on purpose—like maybe to make whatever it was you said more clever than it actually was. And you might do it by accident—like you forget the exact word somebody used, so you substitute another one temporarily, and later you can't remember which was the real word and which was the substitute.

So I can't tell you for sure what really happened. But what I remember about Dad leaving Mom is that it was strange when he wasn't there to tuck me in, and stranger when he wasn't there the next morning. And I remember that my mom's eyes were red, but I didn't connect that with being sad because I didn't know yet that grown-ups cried. And Mom must have been trying really hard to keep things happy because she made pancakes for breakfast even though it wasn't a weekend, and she put a canned-fruit smiley face on top—a pineapple slice smile, cherry nose, mandarin orange eyebrows.

(That part almost has to be made up because since when does my mom keep all that stuff in the cupboard? Or did she keep it in the cupboard in those days? In those days, was she much different than she is now? Was she different when she was still married to my dad?)

After that, she put on music and let me dance on top of the coffee table, which was my number one favorite thing to do, usually something I could only do when I had an especially clueless baby-sitter.

My mom called me to the phone. My dad said, "Sunshine? Now, I don't want you to worry about anything. I'm right here, and I'll call every day."

I said, "Right where? When are you coming home? What are you bringing me?"

Dad laughed. It sounded loud. He said, "What would you like, sunshine? Would you like some new dress-up clothes? How would that be? Maybe a ballerina costume? What are those things called—a tutu?"

I said, "I want lipstick." I was testing. Daddy was gone, which was strange. Maybe other things were strange, too. Maybe the normal rules of life had been canceled. If so, would I finally get lipstick? Before, they would never buy it for me. They said it was for big girls only, and I wasn't quite big enough. They said I would draw on the walls.

Dad laughed his new loud laugh. He said, "Lipstick— we'll have to see about."

I asked him again, "When are you coming home?"

He didn't answer right away, and in the pause before he did, I heard a woman's voice. Did the voice really say "sweet-heart," or is that a memory I added later—like after I found out that my dad had left my mom to be with Rita? Did my dad really call me from Rita's apartment that day? How tacky is that—the day after you leave your wife, you call your three-year-old daughter from your girlfriend's apartment?

Or maybe there wasn't a woman's voice at all. Maybe I added that part, too.

But in the end, does it matter if my dad was nine points

tacky or only five points? He left. And eventually he left Rita, too. He has had girlfriends since, but he doesn't marry them anymore, which my mom says might be a sign he is maturing. He lives by himself in a small white house that needs paint. There is a spare bedroom for me. I used to go there a lot—almost every weekend—but now it's more like once a month.

He said, "I'm not coming home, sunshine," and his voice stuck for a second, which might have meant he was thinking of crying. He said, "But I'll see you very soon. And we'll get some lipstick, too. Would you like that? We'll go to the drugstore. Okay? Any color you want. But now I have to go. I'll talk to you tomorrow, I promise."

I said, "Daddy? Are you a long way away?"

But I said that to the air because he had already hung up.

Chapter Twenty-two

Reason Twenty-two: Because when you think about the things you might want from a boy that you don't get from a girl, other than kissing and the other physical junk, what is there?

You probably remember that my first-ever date ended with me asking Elliot, oh so articulately, "See you at work?"

That was on a Sunday night. And what do you know—the Wednesday after that, we did see each other at work. We were both on an after-school shift, four to close.

If I were going to rewrite my memory of Monday and Tuesday to make myself a better person, I would claim that I had barely thought about Elliot at all. I had many more important things to think about. Like . . . uh . . . well there was an AP European History test, I think, and we were reading *Hamlet* in English.

But the truth, unfortunately, is that I am not a good person, I am only Jane, and in those couple of days, I pretty much thought about Elliot five times a minute. I replayed the night we went to Tivoli, his rescuing Tiffany from Mr. Black, our walk home in the rain. And then I wondered if he was doing the same thing. And did he like kissing me as much as I liked kissing him? Was he mad that I wouldn't let him unhook my bra? Did he want to see me again—even though I'm so "inexperienced"?

When finally he came into work that afternoon, it was weird, like he had stepped right out of my head. At first he was friendly—smiled at me across the tub of pickles—but then when we were six inches apart and sweating while we waited for a space to clear on the giant, rotating bagel toaster, he ignored me totally and talked to Robbie.

My mood soared and plummeted in sync with Elliot's smiles and frowns. If there were a picture of my brain activity during that shift, it would show me half the time agonizing about what was going on in Elliot's head and half the time getting mad at myself for agonizing about what was going on in Elliot's head.

By the time the doors were locked and the CLOSED sign was in the window, I was exhausted. Witch Lady had gone home already—another one of her headaches, I think—and only Elliot, Liz, and I were left. Elliot had the keys, which meant he was in charge. Actually, Liz has been working at Seymour's longer, plus she's older, a sophomore at the university, but Witch Lady would never put her in charge. In fact, Witch Lady fires Liz about once a week. Somehow, though, Liz is always back to work her next shift.

Liz was mopping the floor behind the sandwich counter, and she tripped over the suds bucket, which sloshed a big, dirty, fast-moving puddle. I didn't notice this till she said, "Oh, shoot," and when I looked over, she was standing there watching the puddle expand, like it was some act of nature no mere human being could stop. I grabbed a dry rag from the cleaning cart and knelt on the floor to sop up the mess. Liz helped by pointing out soap bubbles I had missed.

When I stood up, I noticed how pale she was, the bluish hollows under her eyes. It's a wonder she had survived her shift. None of this was unusual, though. Liz leads a wild life, and even more than living it, she likes to tell us younger kids—"littles" she calls us—about it. Working with Liz, I have heard more than I wanted to know about fraternity parties, ways to combine alcohol into tasty and colorful beverages, guys she hooks up with, and even once, in detail, what she and the guy du jour did. I am not sure, but maybe this is good for my education. She says it is. She says it is her responsibility to warn us littles about college life.

She says, "Don't follow my example. Take care of yourselves."

I took the mop from her and told her to sit down. She said, "Thanks, little. You're a pal."

I wiped the sandwich counter, and Elliot emerged from below. He was restocking the walk-in, and his arms were loaded with Ziploc bags of shredded lettuce. He smiled at me and asked if everything was okay, and my mood soared again—*this is so embarrassing even to remember*—and I wanted to say how could there be anything in the universe that is not okay when you are smiling that way at me, but of course, I didn't say that.

I said, "Fine. We're almost done."

He said, "Looks like one of you is altogether done."

Liz stuck her tongue out and said, "If he knew what happened to me last night—"

I said, "Why don't you go to bed early tonight?"

She said, "I might miss something."

I said, "Missing something might be healthy."

Liz said, "Oh, little, you are such a mother, and I mean that in a nice way."

Elliot rolled the cleaning cart out. All that was left was wiping down the tables. He looked at Liz and said, "Go home. Junebug and I will finish up."

Junebug?

"Are you sure?" she asked.

"You're no help," Elliot said.

Liz nodded. "True."

Elliot unlocked the door to let her out. She waved as she walked by the front window. Wherever she was going, it wasn't home. Her apartment is in the other direction.

Elliot got a rag from the cart and the spray bottle, and went to work.

This was the first time we had been alone together since we went to Tivoli, a moment I had been daydreaming about. He didn't have to swoop me up in his arms exactly, but he might at least have said some normal, nice something about how crazy Liz was or what a shame it was that Panacho was opening down the street. But he didn't say a word.

Mood of Jane? Plummeting.

Plus, what was that "Junebug" business? Had he forgotten my name?

So I wiped down some tables myself. And then I felt his eyes on me. He had stopped working.

I looked up. He was wearing his white Seymour's T-shirt and a pair of jeans the faded blue of his eyes. A lock of his blond hair drooped across his forehead. His face was more than friendly—it was affectionate. He looked so good, I had to lean against a table to stay on my feet. I said, "What?" and I was amazed at how normal my voice sounded.

"Alone at last," he said. "Junebug."

After that it was official. He called me Junebug. We were going out.

Chapter Twenty-three

Reason Twenty-three: Because after you break up, every place you look, you'll see something that reminds you of him.

Last week I found a stale pink jelly bean stuck to the bottom of my wastebasket, and all of a sudden it was Easter again and I was making Elliot a white-sugar egg, the old-fashioned kind where there's a scene inside and you look through an opening at one end to see it. The directions were on the back of a cereal box. For the scene I cut a bunny silhouette out of yellow construction paper, glued him with frosting onto green-dyed coconut grass, and surrounded him with jelly beans. It turned out good, and I showed it to Grandma and Bruce and even Mom before I hid it in a basket in Elliot's yard after church on Easter.

Elliot's mom was in on my plan, of course. I had already been to dinner at their house, seen the display case in the living room that is full of Elliot's fencing trophies. By then I had figured out that Elliot was really good, one of the best saber fencers in Pennsylvania. But he was never going to the Olympics or anything. He wasn't rated in the top ten in the age group nationwide, and you would pretty much have to be by now if you think you're going to the Olympics.

I had looked all this up online. I wanted to be able to talk to Elliot about fencing without sounding like an idiot.

But after that it sometimes seemed like Elliot wished I hadn't looked it up. It meant he wasn't the only authority on the subject, and I don't know, did he think maybe my admiration was different because I knew how good he was, and how good he wasn't?

The first time I went to dinner at his house, Elliot showed me the display case, and he looked down at me and smiled a slightly embarrassed smile. Did I mention he has very white teeth? The kind of clean teeth you don't mind getting to know intimately?

He said, "My mom. She thinks I'm wonderful. Who am I to argue?"

Elliot's mom is named Denise. She made us lasagna. She is very short, and his dad—who lives in Ohio with what Elliot calls the new, improved wife and the new, improved kids—is very tall. Elliot's dad played basketball in college, so obviously that's where Elliot got his height and maybe his coordination, too. From his mom he got only his slightly pointy nose.

Elliot says his parents were married for about half an hour.

I have to say one thing about Elliot and me, we did fit right together—we looked good together. That mattered to me, which I guess means I'm shallow. Amy says so, at least. She says this so emphatically that I wonder if Tony, the sexy bassoon player from Golden Eagle, is a dwarf or has funky hair or a wart on his nose or something. Anyway, it's like every single day that I'm reminded how Elliot and I looked good—every time

I'm even in my room—because on my dresser is a framed photograph of him and me with Stacy and Kevin before the prom.

Amy had to miss it this year because it was the same weekend the jazz band went to New York to compete. I wouldn't have missed it for anything. I had never been to one before, and my family went over to Stacy's house for pictures before dinner. John even met us there so he could snap a couple, and my dad came from Pleasant Haven. Dad had bought a new digital camera for the occasion.

I look at that picture—and I remember a lot of things, like how uncomfortable my shoes were, sandals with two-inch heels. Usually I never wear high heels because they make me as tall as an Amazon, but in College Springs you don't exactly go to the prom in flip-flops. We took the pictures in the garden, and the dirt was soft, and my right heel sank in, and I nearly broke my ankle. I thought it would swell up and I'd spend the evening sitting in a chair with an ice pack made out of napkins—but in about five minutes it was totally fine.

Kevin, Stacy's ex, is one of those boys who won't dance, so I lent her Elliot a few times, but not too many. I guess I was feeling pretty possessive that night. Elliot is kind of a showy dancer. He's graceful—fencing, again—and he doesn't mind being the center of attention. For once in my life, when we were dancing, I didn't mind being the center of attention, either.

Something you would probably notice in the picture on my dresser—Stacy is wearing a wrist corsage, but I'm not. Elliot didn't buy me one. He was saving for the fencing uniform. He did shell out to rent a tux, though, and I remember the all over pleasure I felt when he came to the door, when I saw how gorgeous he looked. Even my mom said he was handsome.

The jelly bean in the wastebasket. The photo on my dresser. And this morning I discover not even my underwear drawer is safe. I am digging through before work, trying to find the only bra I own that I actually like, and I pull out the pathetic limp remains of a daffodil Elliot picked for me in April.

We had been walking on the path that goes around the university golf course. The poor lonely flower was back in the trees, deprived of sunlight, the last daffodil to bloom in Pennsylvania this spring. Elliot bent down to break the stalk, and I protested, but he said, "Who would even see it back here besides us?"

Then he knelt on one knee and presented it to me. "And who would ever appreciate it more than you, my Lady Jane?"

He had, like, a way about him. He was different, more sophisticated than other boys. The first fencing match I went to, he won his bout, and later he told me his win was dedicated to me, and he presented me with the ribbon—another mine in the memory minefield because I tacked it on the bulletin board on my bedroom door, and I didn't even notice it there till last week.

I ripped the ribbon off my door and threw it away. I threw the daffodil away, too, and I flushed the jelly bean down the toilet.

And each thing I discarded—it was like discarding part of myself.

I guess that sounds totally stupid.

But it's another one of the weird things about a relationship ending. When the person who loved you doesn't love you anymore—is all the stuff he said erased? He doesn't think you're cute anymore, or smart anymore, or sexy anymore—so now you're not? When a relationship ends, you feel a little like Cinderella at midnight. All the magic that surrounded you, that made you special—all the magic has worn off.

And what's left is the photo of us at the prom. And that stays on my dresser because for a picture that includes me, it's not so bad. It's kind of the way I want to think I look—only, as Grandma might say, cleaned up a bit. My dress is rose-colored with a fitted bodice and a flowing skirt. I'm smiling, but not one of those pasted-on smiles like always happen in school pictures. I just look happy. I *was* happy.

Chapter Twenty-four

Reason Twenty-four: Because boys never learn.

Remember how I have this theory that maybe there are different ways of remembering stories from your life? Like when you remember things, you might change them to make the story better or to make yourself happier?

That last section—that's one way to tell the story of me and Elliot. It's all true, too—I swear.

But there are other ways to tell that story too.

Like when we were walking around the golf course that time? He gave me the daffodil, and then he said, "You know, Junebug, it's pretty secluded back here. I haven't seen another person in half an hour, have you?" And then he put his arms around me, which would have been fine—wonderful—except that I knew what was coming, the wrestling match that more or less defined me and Elliot, the wrestling match that eventually—with a little help from Mrs. Bose and Mom—caused us to break up.

I know what you're thinking.

Jane the Goodie-Good. Jane the Eternal Virgin. Jane the Ice Queen.

Jane the Idiot Who Didn't Take Advantage of a Very Good Thing When It Was Offered.

I know because I thought all that, too. I know because Elliot pointed it all out to me. I know because I talked it out to the last apostrophe, comma, and exclamation point with Stacy and Amy, and they both said, "Never do anything you don't want to do, Jane." But at the same time, I felt like neither one of them could quite figure out why I didn't want to do it.

The second time Elliot and I went out, we parked in the dark by the soccer field, and he said, "We can take this slow. I don't want to scare you."

But even after he said that, I was always the brakes.

So you're asking for details? Gruesome details?

Yeah, he took my bra off, and yeah, he put his hands down my jeans, and yeah—when he did, he had my permission.

Like I would have stayed with him another second if he didn't.

And finally the whole thing got to be kind of ridiculous. So by the millionth time he said, "Why not?" I had run out of good answers.

We were on the sofa at his house. I was half-undressed. He had the sweetest, most tender expression on his face, and I melted.

ME: Okay.

ELLIOT: Okay, what?

ME: *Okay,* okay. I mean . . . okay, we can . . . make love.

ELLIOT: *Really?*

ME: Yes. Really.

ELLIOT: Because I don't want you to if you don't want to.

ME: I do want to.

ELLIOT: You don't sound sure that you want to.

ME: I *am* sure.

ELLIOT *(rolls on top of me):* You mean like—right now?

ME: *No!* I mean, no. Not right now. Your mom'll be back in what, like ten minutes?

ELLIOT *(rolls off of me):* If not right now, then I don't think I believe you want to.

ME *(grabs his shoulder): Elliot!* Give me a break. I mean, we're going to do this . . . thing, this thing that to me is a *big* thing, and it'll be all rushed, and then like: "Oh, hi, Mom."

ELLIOT *(sighs):* Okay. Good point. So when? I mean—are you sure you want to? *Why* do you want to?

ME: Uh . . . because you do, I guess.

ELLIOT: That's not a good reason.

ME *(exasperated):* Elliot! This isn't fair. You have been begging me, and finally I say okay, only now "okay" isn't good enough.

ELLIOT *(retrieves T-shirt from floor, sits up, pulls T-shirt over head):* Why "okay" *now?*

ME *(still exasperated):* Because it will be good! Because I love you! Because I'm ready!

Elliot smiled. He sighed. He said, "Oh, Junebug." He was sitting up, and I was lying down. He looked at me like I was beautiful, and his expression was soft, and he said, "It will be good. I promise. I know what I'm doing. I'll take care of you. I'll get the protection."

And we made a plan for the party at Stacy's, July 22— when her parents were going to Atlantic City for a conference.

Chapter Twenty-five

Reason Twenty-five: Because boys make jokes even when you're serious.

I hope you won't be too disappointed when I tell you that even with her parents gone, Stacy's parties are not that wild. That's because most of our friends are boring and responsible. They run cross-country instead of playing football. They play in the chamber ensemble instead of in a rock band. They're on student council instead of the homecoming court.

To a boring, responsible kid here in College Springs, *bad* means drinking more than one beer, buying cigarettes at the mini-mart, or failing to study for a bio test.

Do anything a lot worse than that and . . . well . . . I guess you get invited to different parties.

So what we mostly do at Stacy's is play music loud, eat junk, watch movies we've watched one thousand times already, play Twister, drink beer or soda or—sometimes—weird concoctions mixed up from the liquor cabinet, and make out in whatever bedroom or corner is available.

Up till this particular party all my personal experience with the making-out part consisted of walking in on other people. I seem to have almost an instinct for doing that. Everybody's used to it by now. They say, "Oh, it's okay. Just Jane again." And then they proceed with what they're doing, and I scurry backward as quietly as possible, blushing miserably.

But that night was going to be different. Of course, Stacy and Amy were totally up-to-date, and Stacy had even reserved me the best bedroom—not her parents', that was always off-limits, but the guest room with the antique bed.

Memories get polluted. If I could look back on the early part of that evening, see it clearly, it would be beautiful. Beautiful is how it was at the time. But now I know what happened next, and I see the view like I'm seeing it through smog.

Elliot came to my door wearing cargo shorts and a yellow polo shirt. He was also wearing body spray, or maybe it was aftershave. He had never put stuff like that on before. I knew he was trying to please me, but it kind of had the opposite effect. It made him seem more, I don't know, *alien,* maybe? Not like from another planet, like a stranger.

But he was so sweet, held my hand walking to Stacy's, told me how cute I was, told me he loved me.

Not that he hadn't said "I love you" before, but it had always been more the way you'd say "thank you" after somebody passed the peas—because it was the thing you say. That night, as we walked in the twilight, he looked into my eyes and said "I love you" like he meant it.

For days all I'd thought about was what was coming later, what it would be like—one of those gauzy love scenes from a movie where the light's all golden and the flesh is all honey-colored?

Would I hear violins?

See fireworks?

Would it hurt?

I know I sound clueless, but actually Stacy and Amy had done their best to fill me in. Stacy even told me not to worry about the sheets, because Luisa—she cleans their house—has every kind of laundry product.

Amy said we might want Kleenex, and it was a good thing there was a bathroom off the guest room.

"It might not be romantic at all," Stacy warned. "It might be like one of those stupid comedies where everything goes wrong. Like all the, you know, *plumbing*—it misfires?"

But I thought that would be okay, too—as long as Elliot looked at me at the end and said he loved me. As long as we were laughing together, not one laughing at the other—specifically, not *him* laughing at *me*.

Stacy lives on the other side of the college campus. On our way Elliot and I stopped downtown at McCracken's Grocery and picked up taco chips and salsa. That's like the unofficial cover charge for attending a party. The slightly more ambitious alternative is usually a pan of brownies made from a mix, but when we got to Stacy's, I saw some really creative person had brought a box of Panacho raspberry–chocolate chip swirl bagels. The ones with the pink frosting? I remember I felt a burst of sympathy for Mr. Black's mission. I mean, it's obvious there's nothing dangerous about a date nut bagel, but raspberry–chocolate chip swirl?

For a long time after we got there, I didn't actually see that much of Elliot. I think he was playing poker with a bunch of guys on the floor in the hallway outside Stacy's parents' room.

He had this idea he was pretty good at it and maybe he'd make some money toward the fencing uniform.

Our plan was to meet at midnight outside the guest bedroom. In summer my curfew is twelve, but I was staying over at Stacy's. Mom didn't know Stacy's parents were away, and she hadn't asked for details when I went out. Not getting asked a lot of questions is a byproduct of being—most of the time— a good and responsible kid.

At five minutes to midnight, I tore myself away from the basement screening of *The Lion King*—no, I am not kidding—and ran up the stairs. On the way I made a pit stop in the first-floor bathroom, following more wise advice from practical Amy. When I washed my hands, I almost couldn't look at myself in the mirror, I was so afraid I'd find an emerging zit or other horror to destroy my confidence. But finally when I did peek, I looked okay. I wondered if I would look different in the morning.

Elliot was there waiting for me. In a moment, I was in his arms, and in the next, he had spun me into the bedroom. The door closed with a click. I was surprised to realize that I was breathing hard, my pulse racing.

"Oh, Junebug," Elliot whispered in my ear, "this is going to be so good. You are so cute."

Then—without further ado—he scooped me up, carried me to the bed, laid me down, and went to work removing my clothes. He was surprisingly quick at this. Of course I knew he'd been with other girls. I even knew one of the girls. But had he had that much practice? Or maybe it was just natural aptitude.

When I was good and naked—so much for the fancy underwear I picked out—he looked down at me and smiled. I wasn't *in* the bed but on it, the bedspread cool underneath my bare back and bottom, cool and a little unfriendly, like no one had ever lain on it long enough to soften it up. I shivered. I felt gooseflesh. A thought tried to form—a thought like What are you doing here, Jane?

While Elliot removed his own clothes—an operation that took maybe three seconds—I rolled onto my side and sneaked a glance at myself, expecting to be mortified by how much I *don't* look like the girls in love scenes in movies.

Only I looked okay. My body, which I usually think of as pale and blobby, looked rosy and feminine—each one of my female parts in its appropriate place. I was appealing. I was— maybe—even sexy.

His clothes now mixed up with mine on the floor, Elliot gave me a moment to admire his exactly right boy body. I had seen most of him before, of course, but not the complete . . . package. I guess it's like Amy says. If you grow up in a house without brothers, you aren't prepared for certain things—like the way boys treat a toilet and like that whole between-the-legs boy apparatus, which now appeared before me at eye level in all its prominence and glory.

I mean, *whoa.*

Thankfully, Elliot dropped onto the bed pronto, and then everything, apparatus included, was squished against me.

We had never been naked together before. I was aware of every prickle of his hair tickling my skin, of the little square on his jaw he missed when he was shaving, of his toenails, sharp against my shins. And soon I was aware that all of it was damp—it had been a warm day, and it wasn't long before a layer of sweat slickened us.

"Oh, *baby*," he said, which was weird because he never called me *baby*. I was Junebug or Lady Jane, but not baby.

Was that it?

Or the lime-slush scent of the body spray?

Was it his breath, which smelled like the taco chips we brought to the party?

Should he have slowed down or speeded up or tickled my armpit in some more considerate way?

I have spent more hours dissecting every moment of that night than I spent on AP European History all last year, and I still don't know. The only thing I know is that all of a sudden, everything felt wrong.

And not funny ha-ha wrong; or hey, the plumbing doesn't work; hey, we're-not-very-good-at-this-yet wrong; but truly wrong. And I wished I were anywhere else at all, in my own bed looking at my dad's sunshine on the ceiling. I wished I were *alone*.

"*Elliot!*" I grabbed his wrist. "*Hey—please? Elliot?*"

Elliot's lips and tongue were smashed against some distant part of me, so at first, his response was only a mumble. Finally I had to pull his hair to get his attention. He didn't like that, but it worked.

"*Ow—hey!* Baby, *what?*" he said, and his eyes flashed, but then he caught himself, and his voice dropped. "Did I hurt you?"

I wanted to cry. I wanted to escape. I didn't know what I wanted.

But it wouldn't be fair to stop, would it? We had made a deal.

Only . . . *I didn't want to.*

So I took a deep breath and pushed him away—but not far away—and I tried to explain: "It just doesn't feel right."

And he said, "You don't love me."

"Yes I do!" I said, feeling totally confused and deflated. "I'm sorry. I'm *so* sorry."

And that was the moment I knew it wasn't going to happen. We weren't going to discuss it and then maybe I'd change my mind. It wasn't going to happen.

Elliot was leaning his head on his elbow and staring right into my eyes. His face was blank, no expression at all. His blue eyes, ordinarily so hot, were icy.

He said, "Just get dressed, Jane."

Chapter Twenty-six

Reason Twenty-six: Because even the mere idea of boys is hard on your driving skills.

I was supposed to stay over at Stacy's, but the party was still going on when I came downstairs, and I couldn't face live human beings, so I decided to go home. I would have walked, which wouldn't have been especially smart at that time of night—even in dinky College Springs. Luckily, Stacy spotted me before I got to the door.

"What's the matter?" she asked.

"Do I look really bad?"

"Uh . . . yeah."

I didn't want to talk about it, but she saw it was serious and said hold on, she would drive me.

"But . . . your party?" I said.

"My party will still be here," she said.

I scrutinized her a second, and she read my mind. "And *no*, not even a single beer," she said. "Somebody's got to keep order, right?"

In the car she tried to make me laugh by telling funny stories about our friends. When I didn't laugh, she gave up.

"When you want to talk, call me," she said when we got to my house.

"I'm going to my dad's tomorrow."

"So call me," she said again.

I slipped in the front door as quietly as I could. I didn't know for sure what time it was but way after my curfew, obviously. I tiptoed toward the stairs and halfway there kicked an empty paint can. The sound was like a gong echoing through the house. Thanks so much, Very-Nice Construction, I thought. And I waited for my mom's light to go on, for her to appear at the top of the stairs and ask what I meant by being so late.

But she didn't.

Was it possible she hadn't heard?

I waited another minute—still no Mom.

She must be really sound asleep, I thought. One lucky thing on this so unlucky night.

You know how when you burn yourself, at first you don't feel it?

What happened with Elliot that night was like a burn, and for a while, I was just numb. It's like I knew if I allowed myself to feel it totally, it was gonna hurt like crazy.

So I went to sleep. And it wasn't till the next morning that the anxiety kicked in. That last look Elliot laid on me—was that what he was feeling *now*, too?

Maybe I should have gone through with it.

And if I had, how would I be feeling now?

Maybe I'd be looking back on a wonderful dreamy experience, feeling closer to Elliot than ever, more in love than ever—bonded.

But something—that same doubt from last night—told me no, I wouldn't feel that way at all.

My head was spinning, and I guess I must have drifted off to sleep again because the next thing I knew, my mom was shaking me.

"Sweetie? I thought you were staying at Stacy's?"

"Hi . . . uh . . . no," I mumbled. "That didn't work out."

"Well, I'm sorry to rush you," she said, "but I've got to get you to your dad's and then be back for an appointment. Are you packed?"

I didn't want to pack. I wanted to get on IM and see if Elliot was on. I wanted to check my cell phone for messages, my e-mail for some comforting little note. I wanted to find out if after last night, my boyfriend hated me and was dumping me—or what.

But instead, I performed Jane's Famous Not-Thinking Trick, and a few minutes later I was up and dressed and gathering underwear, shorts, T-shirts, and a toothbrush for the overnight at Dad's.

Mom appeared again in my doorway.

"You know, we really ought to practice your driving," she said. "Otherwise, you're never going to get your license. The learner's permit requires—"

"—Fifty hours, Mom. Like I don't know." I was crabby.

"Jane, look. I know you're reluctant about driving, but it will be a huge help to me when—"

"Mom, do you know how many people die on the highway every day?"

"Jane, do you know how many people *don't*?" she said. "You can't be independent if you don't drive. So . . . you're driving us to your dad's today."

Oh, this was just great. I was sleepless and anxious and distracted—and now I was going to be operating a potentially lethal one-ton piece of machinery. But I couldn't explain to my mom *why* this was such an especially bad idea today. That was the last thing I wanted to talk about. So I took the keys from her and followed her down the stairs—skirting the paint can I kicked last night—and out the front door.

Our old Toyota was in the driveway, and as I walked toward it I saw Ashok and his mom were leaving their house, too.

"Good morning, Cynthia! Good morning, Jane!" Mrs. Bose called, and like a heat-seeking missile, she headed toward us, Ashok trailing behind. She was wearing traditional Indian dress, a red and yellow sari. Usually to teach or work in her lab, she wears western-style pantsuits, but when the weather is hot, she wears saris.

"Good morning, Neena," my mother said, and I winked at Ashok, who was remaining in the background. I think Ashok winked back, but it might have been only that the sun was in his eyes. I don't think Ashok gets a lot of practice winking.

The two moms started in on some mom babble; topic A was our remodeling, as usual. I would have liked to talk to Ashok, but I felt shy about walking over to him, afraid the moms might make something big out of it.

So instead, I zoned out, the sun making me sleepy, till I heard my name.

"Huh?" I woke up. "I'm sorry, Mrs. Bose. What?"

"I said, I'm not surprised you're looking so drowsy, Jane. By the kitchen clock it was after two when you came in last night."

Mom looked at me. "Oh, really, Jane?"

It is poor policy to lie. I know this. But sometimes when you're startled, lying is a reflex, like blinking at a camera flash.

"Oh, I don't *think* so, Mrs. Bose. I'm really careful about my curfew."

"No, no, Jane, I am quite certain about the time," she said. "I was in the kitchen for a glass of water, you see, and when I got back to bed, I double-checked on my clock radio. It's a Sony, very accurate."

Ashok's expression said he would be stuffing a gag in his mom's mouth only he didn't happen to have a gag handy. Short of inventing some story about Martians changing the clocks, I couldn't think of an argument, so I just said, "Interesting. Well, Mom, don't we have to go?"

"Yes, we should," Mom said. "Always a pleasure to talk to you, Neena. Nice to see you, Ashok. When did you get so handsome, anyway?"

In the car my mom didn't say anything about my curfew, so I didn't either. Besides, driving took all my concentration.

My mom's idea of teaching me is to put on this goopy voice and coo praise every time I turn a corner without flattening anybody. I would tell her to save it, but I am usually too busy missing the obstacles that pop up in front of me—kind of the way they do in video games.

I was only a couple of blocks from home when an enormous gray garbage truck appeared from nowhere on my left, and I had no idea what to do. Speed up? Slow down? Dodge it?

And my mom said, "Keep right on going, honey. You have the right-of-way."

And I imagined the inscription on my tombstone: SHE HAD THE RIGHT-OF-WAY.

The driving got easier out on the highway. All I had to do was not think how likely it was that deer, antelope, and cows might suddenly leap in front of us, and then there was always the chance of fishtailing big rigs and sudden blinding snow storms.

I had just determined that the odds were slightly in favor of us arriving at my dad's alive—and because of that my pulse rate was dropping into the normal zone—when my mom finally brought up the time I got home last night.

"You were out with Elliot, weren't you?" she asked. "Do I need to give you the little talk?"

"What little talk?" I asked, successfully avoiding a row of mailboxes on the right. Why do people build mailboxes so close to the highway, anyway?

"Steady there," Mom said. "The little talk about not getting pregnant and not getting sick."

"You did that when I was like ten!" I said.

"You might need a refresher," she said, "especially if you're going to be out half the night with a boy."

There was no point claiming Mrs. Bose couldn't read a clock. So I said, "Till two is not half the night."

"It's two hours beyond your curfew, Jane. And when you violate the rules, there are consequences."

A very sincere-sounding apology might have gotten me time off for good behavior. But I was sleepy and mad about being caught and mad about driving to my dad's and mad about being scared to drive to my dad's, so I didn't say anything. After a few more tense moments Mom said, "You're grounded for a week, Jane. That means no going out except for work."

"A *week*!" I said. "But Tuesday is Elliot's and my four-month anniversary! He has a match in Lewisville, and I promised—"

"You should have thought of that before you stayed out past your curfew," she said.

I tried logic. "Mom, if I had stayed at Stacy's overnight, I wouldn't have been home till morning!"

Mom was not impressed. "You should have stayed at Stacy's, then," she said. "Why didn't you?"

I wasn't going to answer that one. Instead, I surprised myself by successfully maneuvering the car off the highway and down the Pleasant Haven off-ramp. A block later we pulled up in front of my dad's house.

I had my hand on the door handle when Mom said, "And I think it might be a good idea if you didn't contact Elliot this weekend, either."

"What?" I said. *"Why?"*

"Because I think it would be a good idea. Jane, listen. You're getting a little too dependent on him, spending a little too much time, don't you think? That's risky at your age. You want to be seeing a *variety* of people, boys and girls. . . ." And off she went on Mom Speech no. 127, one of the endless variations of Why You Have to Give Back Josh Silberman's Star of David.

Chapter Twenty-seven

Reason Twenty-seven: Because men and women are fundamentally incompatible.

Nobody ever sat down to tell me The Rise and Fall of the Romance of Jane's Parents, but after a while, from talking to them and to Grandma, I more or less pieced it together. This is what happened:

They met when they were sophomores at the university. Mom was premed, and Dad was an English major with no educational plan except to keep a C average so his parents back in Pittsburgh would keep supporting him. What Dad really cared about was music, especially his band, Narcoleptic Sparrow. He was the lead guitarist and the lead singer, also the main songwriter. Mom saw him play at a local club and— this is how she says it—she fell in love after the first chord progression.

"I don't know what it was," she told me once, "but you put a guy on a stage with a mike and a spotlight—it's not like he even needs to have that much talent—he's instantly special."

"You mean, like, he's a rock star?" I said.

She had laughed. "Yeah, exactly like that."

I could kind of relate. Up till Elliot came along, the most serious love interest in my life had been Scissors, bass guitarist for Bomb-Sniffing Dogs. But I never expected Scissors to step off the stage one night and offer to buy me a beer. That's what my dad did for my mom—and it was their first date, I guess, and the next thing you know, Mom was spending more time following Narcoleptic Sparrow than she was on organic chemistry.

So much for premed. She switched majors to something less competitive, library science. When they graduated—and Dad's parents announced he was on his own—they got married and moved in together mostly to save money, and she got a job as a "deputy assistant to the deputy assistant librarian" at the county library in Belletoona. I don't think there really is such a job, but she always says it that way to emphasize how pathetic it was. Dad tried to make money playing music, but when Mom got pregnant with me, he decided to get serious and get a teaching credential.

I was born. He graduated. He got a job at Pleasant Haven Middle School—the same job he still has. But at night he still played clubs sometimes, and there were other girls who had the same reaction to him my mom did. Dad is not the best at resisting temptation. If you doubt that, take a look at his ever-expanding tummy.

"Your father," my grandmother told me once, "was never really marriage material. And to be fair, your mother can be a bit of a martinet."

I always worry when I hear a word I don't know. I have been studying vocab for the SAT for pretty much ever. I should know *all* the words by now. "What is a martinet?" I asked Grandma.

"It means demanding and unyielding," Grandma said.

I agreed. Mom can be a martinet.

"So in comparison, Rita probably looked good," Grandma said.

"That doesn't make it right that he left us," I pointed out.

"No, it doesn't, honey," said Grandma, "but maybe understandable."

You might think I would've been too upset to see straight when I departed Mom and the Toyota, when I made a break for my dad's door. But sometimes it's surprising what a person notices—like how my dad's front walk was overgrown with weeds and how there were more dandelions than anything else in what were supposed to be flower beds. It's all pretty different from Mom's and my house, especially from how it's going to be when Very-Nice Construction finishes the remodel—if they ever do, that is.

I guess it makes sense, though. My dad and mom are so totally different. My dad says gardening is for people who never discovered the finer things—like rock 'n' roll and poetry. He doesn't have a lot of respect for cooking and cleaning, either. A gourmet meal from my dad is when he sprinkles frozen peas in with the ramen noodles.

Also, even though my dad makes an okay salary teaching, he never has any money. He has to pay child support for his darling daughter, of course, and he takes whatever is left and buys guitars. If that sounds crazy to you, you don't know any musicians. At last count my dad had fifteen guitars, and he really wants one more—a pre-CBS Stratocaster, just like Jimi

Hendrix played. He swears, if he can only get one, he will never buy another guitar. I told my mom that, and she just laughed.

I burst through the front door and hollered, "Daddy? Hi!" He came into the living room wiping his hands on a dish towel, which meant he had been trying to wash a week's worth of dirty dishes in time for my arrival.

"Hello, sunshine, is your mom coming in?" he asked.

"I don't know," I said. "She's mad at me."

He said, "Uh-oh. What did you do?"

Before I could answer, the front door opened, and in came Mom. "Hello?"

"Great," I said, and like a brat, I stomped up the stairs to my room.

You couldn't exactly call my parents friends, but the fight burned out of them a long time ago, and most of the time they are polite to each other, even nice. Like, for example, my dad always makes sure I do something for my mom for Mother's Day, and the other way around.

Now, though, I wondered if maybe they would fight over *me*. Would my mom tell my dad I had turned all defiant and boy crazy? Would my dad defend me? Or would he and my mom gang up on me? I wondered if that was how it was for kids whose parents stayed married to each other, which right then seemed like it would be pretty much a nightmare.

I waited upstairs till after my mom called, "Good-bye, Jane!" and left.

When I came down, Dad was in the kitchen making peanut butter sandwiches. "Your mother seems to think you'll try to get in touch with this poet fellow while you're here," he said.

"Poet fellow?"

"Ezra? Rupert? Dylan?" Dad said.

Then I got it. "You're hilarious, Dad. And it's *Elliot.*"

Dad handed me my sandwich. He put it on a piece of paper towel so he wouldn't have to go to the trouble of washing a plate later. He shoved aside *Guitar Player* magazine and a pile of junk mail so there would be space for my sandwich at the kitchen table.

Then he started to quote some poetry, which I guess was written by the poet T. S. Eliot. It was something about Michelangelo. He likes to show off that way, and if I'm in a good mood, I like to listen; but I was not in a good mood, so I ignored him and ate.

Finally he said, "So, are you?"

I said, "Am I what?"

"Are you going to call Elliot—or text him—while you're here?"

I reminded myself I was mad at my mom, not my dad. I said, "Could I have some milk?"

He said, "I wouldn't chance it," which meant he had milk but it was so old, it was probably sour.

I got water for both of us. Then I said, "What if Elliot calls *me* or sends a message?"

"Well, let's just see if he does, shall we? Cross that bridge, and so on?" Dad said. "You've come here other weekends without his calling. I seem to remember this has caused no little consternation in the past."

"Fine," I snapped. "I won't call him."

The rest of the day went like most visits with my dad. When I was little, he used to like to take me on what he called field trips, like to Gettysburg or underground caverns or berry picking. Then I went through a phase—middle school—where I was too embarrassed even to be seen in public with my *dad*, and we mostly stayed in and read books or watched movies. I've kind of grown out of that, so in the afternoon we took a hike at Gompers State Park and argued about *Hamlet*, which I read for English this year. I said Ophelia's death was the saddest part, but he said that couldn't be true because if it was, the play would be called *Ophelia*.

Later we got a pizza and watched *A Day at the Races*. We have seen it a thousand times. It still cracks us up.

The whole time I was a little bored, and probably Dad was, too, but we never said it.

Elliot didn't call or text. This might sound weird, but like my dad said, it wasn't that unusual. Elliot had the match on Tuesday, and his coach was always telling them that before a match they had to be all about focus, no distractions, especially not "lady friends," as he says it. He's Russian, remember, and his English is creative sometimes.

Of course, after what happened at Stacy's, I was dying to know what Elliot was thinking. At the same time, part of me was relieved not to be in touch with him. Part of me was still feeling burned, still didn't want to deal with something that might hurt a lot. Being at Dad's was like a vacation from that.

And besides, I knew we'd talk Tuesday morning when our Seymour's shifts overlapped.

After the movie I was sitting on my bed reading when my cell rang, and it was Stacy. Shoot.

ME: I'm sorry. I know I said I'd call, but—

STACY: Don't worry about it. How *are* you?

ME: Terrible. Fine . . . *fine.*

STACY: Have you talked to . . . you know?

ME: You can use his name, Stace. And no, I haven't. My mom grounded me and said I can't call him.

STACY: And he hasn't called *you?*

ME: He's got a match this week. You know.

STACY: Right.

ME: Seriously.

STACY: Okay, sure. But Jane, come on, what happened?

ME: I don't think I'm ready to talk about it.

STACY: Right. Uh . . . so, how's the weather in Pleasant Haven?

ME: Okay, fine, I'll talk about it.

STACY: Did it happen? I mean, not to be blunt or anything, but I guess that's the question.

ME: Okay, well . . . short answer? No. I . . . uh . . . I wimped out.

STACY: Don't say you wimped out! You made a choice . . . uh . . . didn't you? I mean, unless he . . . I mean, is that what happened? You decided *no?*

ME: I feel bad. I feel like I broke a promise.

STACY: Now you just cut that out, Jane! You are totally a *noodle* if you think that. You changed your mind. Women are allowed to do that. Like, to quote Jane Greene: "You can look it up." And besides, honestly? I am, like, totally relieved.

ME: Relieved?

STACY: Because you looked like the walking green-zombie dead when I took you home last night, and if it was your first time, that would mean you're really unhappy about your first time. But the way it worked out, this is probably something you'll totally forget all about.

ME *(pauses to let this sink in)*: Well, maybe. But right now I'm confused and unhappy, and I feel like I let him down, and—

STACY: Trust Dr. Stacy, Jane. You did the right thing. So don't say that anymore.

ME: Say what anymore?

STACY: That wimped-out thing. I am a woman of experience. I know how these things go. I mean, not to get crude, but at some point it would've been easier just to go along, right?

ME: Right.

STACY: So in actuality, you were *brave*. And besides—

ME: Besides what?

STACY: Elliot's still your boyfriend. It's not like he's going anywhere.

I went home Monday afternoon. Dad asked me if I wanted to drive, and I said no, and he didn't press it. We took the back way, past the old dump. The stink on a July afternoon is bad. You practically have to hold your nose. Nobody was working, but I saw scoopers and the bulldozers lined up, ready to start dredging trash and turning it over the next day.

I said, "Dad, why did you . . . ?"

And then I couldn't quite bring myself to finish the question. So Dad had to say: "Why did I what?" And his voice was light, like I was going to ask about how he always lets the milk go sour and buys cheap peanut butter.

"Why did you leave us?"

And if you're wondering why I asked it then, after all that time . . . well, I'm kind of wondering, too.

Dad laughed the same way he did that first day when he moved out, when he called from Rita's—a loud laugh.

He said, "You know all that, don't you, sunshine? I fell in love with Rita."

That seemed like a cheap answer, so I waited, hoping he'd add to it, but he didn't. We drove past one of the Amish farms, where the farmers don't use regular electricity or motorized vehicles. A woman was bringing in her laundry from the clothesline by the house.

I tried again. "Then why did you leave *her*?"

Dad looked over at me and looked back at the road. He said, "There's no mystery there, sunshine. I fell out of love."

This was exasperating. "*Dad,* love isn't like a—a new guitar! It's not like lipstick or clothes you try on. It's important! You're supposed to stick with it! It's supposed to be for always!"

"Are you thinking of Elliot now?" Dad asked me.

"Not really," I said. "I am more like thinking of Mom and me."

"I don't love you like a new pair of jeans, sunshine," Dad said. "I love you even more than my Martin D-Forty-five."

"I know that," I said. "It's just that . . . you should have stayed with Mom and me."

There. I said it. Then I stole a look over at Dad. He wasn't looking at me. He was looking straight out onto the highway. But he was shaking his head—slowly, like he meant it.

"I'm not proud of leaving the way I did, Jane, but eventually I would have left anyway—or your mom would have. We never would have been happy." There was a pause, then he said, "What happened with Elliot, anyway? You haven't been yourself this visit."

"Everything is *fine* with Elliot," I said.

"You know, sunshine, many critics would disagree," Dad said. "His poetry has been called bloodless and myopic—hidebound in the western tradition."

I sighed. "You're hilarious," I said.

He laughed—a normal laugh this time. "When you live alone," he said, "it's good to be entertained by your own jokes."

Chapter Twenty-eight

Reason Twenty-eight: Because boys don't listen.

I had slept fine at my dad's, but back in my own bed Monday night, I hardly slept at all. I was dissecting what had happened at Stacy's and worrying about how Elliot would be when I saw him at Seymour's bright and early. Of course he had been annoyed and disappointed—but by now? He might still be angry. He might feel guilty, like he had pressured me. He might be so focused on fencing that I barely even blipped on his radar screen.

When I got to work at 6:30 A.M., Witch Lady assigned me to the espresso counter. This was almost as bad as my mom making me drive to my dad's. Espresso is a specialty job. They even give a certificate to peons who pass a test.

"But I haven't trained," I told her.

"I know it, Jane. But Loren's sick, and Shuja won't be in till later. Take a quick look at the employee handbook, and you'll figure it out. Besides, it won't be busy. Panacho has a special going—buy bagels, you get free strawberry cream cheese. It's really taking a bite out of our traffic."

So I took a copy of the employee handbook from Witch Lady's office and installed myself at the espresso counter.

I was reading up on how to tamp the espresso powder when Elliot came up behind me, kissed my neck, and said, "Hey, I missed you. Happy four-month anniversary."

And choirs of angels sang hymns of praise—or anyhow it seemed like it.

"I missed you, too. I'm so . . . uh . . . ," and I was going to say "sorry," but that didn't seem right. I mean, I wasn't exactly sorry. I just felt bad he had been disappointed.

"That's okay," he said, as if I had actually apologized. "There'll be a next time, right?"

I said sure, whether I was or not, and he started to tell me what time I had to be ready for the match that night.

"Oh, Elliot, I am so sorry," I said. "My mom—"

"Your mom what?"

I explained I was grounded.

"But she can't mean my match!" he said. "How will I win without my number one fan?"

I shook my head. "I'm only allowed to come to work. It's like I'm in prison or something."

Elliot had been standing close behind me, the kind of close that means you're going out. Now he took two steps back, and I felt the cool space between us. "I'm not sure I even believe you, Jane," he said.

"What?"

"About your mom. I think you're using her as an excuse."

I said I didn't know what he was talking about.

"I think you do," he said. "Why didn't you call this weekend, anyway?"

"You didn't call either," I said.

145

"Because *you're* the one who had something to apologize for," he said.

I was so surprised, I stammered. "I—I . . . ? I did not!" I thought of my conversation with Stacy. "I just changed my mind. I'm—I'm allowed! Besides, I couldn't call because my mom—"

"Your mom, your mom," Elliot mocked me. "She's just your excuse—an excuse not to come to my match, because you don't really care. Maybe an excuse to break up?"

I turned and faced him, even though it meant my back was to the customers, a violation of Rule Seven of Chapter Three of the employee handbook. "Elliot, you are psycho," I said. "If I wanted to break up with you, I would break up with you. I would not hide behind my mom."

Elliot's only answer was a scowl. Then he turned and walked away.

I felt my face heat up. I was furious and embarrassed. Probably everyone in Seymour's had heard this argument. Liz especially loved this kind of stuff, and she would be sure to give the details to Loren, and Loren would tell anybody else who didn't happen to be in earshot.

I took a deep breath and turned back toward the counter. A pretty woman with a nose ring and spiky black hair was looking at me expectantly. For a second I just stared at her wondering what was she doing here and what did she want from me? Then she said, "Can I get a latte?"

And I snapped out of it. "Welcome to Seymour's. May I help you?"

"Can I get a latte?"

I said, "Yes."

She said, "A double decaf latte with soy milk. And do you have cinnamon? Don't sprinkle it on top, though. Mix it in."

I said, "Sure, no problem."

And then—like it wasn't enough for one day that I had faced Elliot—I had to face the big, hot, hissing espresso machine, too. I spilled the powder. I burned my hand on the steamer. I couldn't find the soy milk at first, and when I did find it, I broke a fingernail trying to open it up.

After what seemed like forty-five minutes I handed the woman her latte.

She asked, "Did you remember to mix in the cinnamon?"

I sighed and took it back. "I'm glad you're not in a hurry," I said.

Later there was this weird postlunch rush at the sandwich counter. Shuja called me over. I hadn't seen Elliot in a while. I thought he must be down in the basement doing prep work—slicing tomatoes and onions, chopping peppers.

My brain felt like a broken radio picking up more than one station, each trying to drown out the others: I should have been heartbroken because Elliot was angry. I should have been mad because Elliot refused to listen to me. I should have been worried because what if he had left me?

I should have been concentrating on sandwiches because I had just spread jam on ham and cheese.

I dropped the inedible sandwich into the trash and pulled another plain bagel out of the bin. Meanwhile, Shuja was saying, "Tomato crisis. Warning! Warning!"

Liz moaned and said, "Oh, jeez, not now. Can one of you littles go? It's too far to walk the way I'm feeling."

Loren said something about how Liz would probably freeze in the walk-in and not be found till spring, and Shuja said, "Probably accurate, Loren, but none of this is getting us tomatoes."

I said, "I'll go," and I slapped the new ham sandwich together, wrapped it, and wrote $4.95 on the paper. Then I said, "Sorry it took so long," for probably the tenth time that afternoon. Then I wiped my hands and walked over to the walk-in for more sliced tomatoes.

Chapter Twenty-nine

Reason Twenty-nine: Because boys waste no time when it comes to revenge.

When you open the walk-in, there is a little *whoosh* of cold, damp, refrigerated air, and immediately you feel goose bumps forming on your skin. I remember how annoyed I was. I didn't want to be cold. I hated the walk-in. Why had I volunteered to go? Wouldn't it be nice if for once Liz did *something*?

But that was as far as I got with being annoyed because all of a sudden I realized I was not alone. The light was dim, so it was the sound that alerted me—people breathing like they were oxygen-deprived. Then I saw two bodies to the right of the door, backed up against the shelves of half-and-half.

Sometimes it takes a person a long time to put facts together.

Heavy breathing. Two bodies.

Oh.

But if it took me, the observer, one long second to recognize what was up, it took them, the participants, at least two seconds to recognize I existed. Then the outside body jerked upright, and the smaller, inside one squealed.

At first I squinched my eyes and blushed, all embarrassed: Jane Walks in on Yet Another Make-out Session.

But I wasn't embarrassed for long, because—like you didn't know—it was Elliot who turned around and looked right at me.

And the smaller, disheveled, girl-type person who was pulling down her T-shirt and wiping his slobber off her face was Valerie.

How long did we stand there? Five seconds? An hour? Anyway, it was long enough that Shuja sent Arthur in to see if maybe frostbite had claimed another victim. I heard the latch click and saw light as the door opened.

Arthur said, "Anybody home? We're suffering a severe tomato famine out here."

Then he, much smarter than me, took in the situation and said, "Earth to Jane? The tomatoes are on the shelf there. Pinkish? Ziploc bags? Pick up a couple and come with me."

I said something oh-so-clever like, "What?" which made Arthur sigh and translate his instructions into even simpler form, suitable for idiots or victims of shock: "Shelf." Pause. "Tomatoes." Pause. "Exit."

When I still didn't move, Arthur reached around me and grabbed the Ziplocs with one hand while steering me toward the door with the other. He said, "Get the latch, Jane. I am fresh out of hands."

This time his words penetrated, and I did as I was told. In a second I was back in the light and the warmth, like I had stepped out of a nightmare. Unfortunately, the nightmare followed right behind. Valerie was too chicken to look up—she skittered like a cockroach into Witch Lady's office. But Elliot was brazen and smug, and the look he shot me was like a six-year-old singing, "Nah-nah-nah-NAH-nah."

Chapter Thirty

Reason Thirty: Because boys cannot even make a cup of tea.

Nine-fifteen A.M., Saturday, August 19. A ray of sunlight shines through my bedroom window and onto my face, annoying me awake. I open one eye, look at my alarm clock, and calculate: It is one week after Mr. Black started working at Seymour's, one week before the Kickoff Parade, and twenty-four days A.E.

The university library is hosting a conference this week-end, so Mom will have left for work already. Very-Nice has the day off—they're stuck waiting until some fancy rock counter-top arrives. For once I am alone in my own house.

I stretch, make a face at Dad's sunshine on the ceiling, and roll over to stare for a few seconds at Trey, Alex, Beau, and Scissors—aka Bomb-Sniffing Dogs—who grin back at me from the poster on my wall.

Mom didn't want me to put the poster back up after my room was painted.

"This band is just a passing fancy with you, Jane. Next week it will be somebody else," she said. "What about that Van Gogh sunflower poster?"

"It's *my* room!" I said.

"But wouldn't you like a more . . . uh . . . *grown-up* look?"

"What is the point in having my own bedroom if I can't decorate it the way I want?"

Eventually, we compromised. She got the Bomb-Sniffing Dogs poster framed and matted in orange to match the Van Gogh sunflowers, which are hanging over my dresser.

Now staring at Trey, Alex, Beau, and Scissors, I realize I pretty much know their every pore and follicle. Not to mention Stacy, Amy, and I have spent many hours discussing each guy's looks. Our conclusions:

1. Beau is the cute one, with a baby face that is just this side of feminine;
2. Trey is soft around the belly and disheveled, like he never got over his little boy's dislike of taking a bath and having his hair combed;
3. Alex has great hair—luxurious afro curls—and a caffe latte complexion; Stacy thinks he's the sexiest, but I think his eyes are too close set;
4. Scissors, my last remaining true love, has olive skin and a sharp nose and intense eyes, like a greaser from the fifties or somebody on *The Sopranos*. I'm the only one who appreciates how attractive he is.

Still facing the poster, I rub my eyes and try to decide if I am sleepy. It's going to be a busy day. I will need plenty of strength to face it. Arthur and I are having soda with Grandma after lunch, then going out to the old barn to work on the Seymour's float. Stacy and Amy will be there, too. Arthur doesn't have to go. He's making some of the costumes, including the sheriff's costume for Seymour. But because we're so late this year, everybody wants to help out. We'll probably be working till late tonight.

Now I can either get up and eat breakfast or—isn't summer wonderful?—close my curtains and sleep for another hour. I am pondering this tough decision when it is made for me. The doorbell rings.

Shoot.

But maybe it's only Mormons or dry cleaning? Maybe if I close my eyes, they will go away?

I close my eyes. The doorbell rings again.

I sit up and look out my window, but a rhododendron bush blocks my view of the door. I don't see a truck on the street. Who could it be?

All right, all right. I'm awake now.

"Jane, I am so sorry." It is Ashok on the front step. He is dressed in shorts, a red T-shirt damp with sweat, and running shoes. "I am locked out of my own house," he says. "Can you believe it? What is that you're wearing? Have you taken up running as well? I am so sorry to disturb you."

I look down at myself and realize I have answered the door in my size XL Pittsburgh Marathon T-shirt. This does not mean I actually have started running yet. It's just that I saw the T-shirt at the thrift shop and figured buying it would be a good first step in my training.

When I realize what I'm wearing, I'm glad it's only Ashok at the door. "Hi . . . uh . . . yeah," I say. "Come in. I wasn't exactly asleep. Do you want to use the phone?"

Ashok explains that he went for a run like he does every morning, and when he came back, his house was locked and his parents were gone. "They must have presumed that I had a key," he says, then he looks around at the chaos that is our downstairs. "What has happened to your house?! Why is the fridge in the living room?"

"You know, Ashok. The remodel?"

"What remodel?"

"The trucks that have been in front of our house for months? The Very-Nice Construction sign in the front yard? The guys who are in and out of here all day?"

Ashok shakes his head. "I did not realize. I am so sorry. It must be very inconvenient to have a fridge in the living room." He points to the phone. "May I?"

I nod. He dials. He waits. He shakes his head. "What a predicament," he says.

"You can stay here as long as you want," I say. "One of them will show up eventually, right? Would you like some coffee? I don't have a kitchen, but I can still make that."

"I have a water bottle, thank you. I don't want to impose."

"You're not imposing," I say.

Ashok grins. "Would it be too much trouble . . . ? I drink tea."

"I can make it in the microwave."

It is surprisingly cozy to fix coffee for myself and tea for Ashok—even without a kitchen. While Ashok dials again, I get tea from the bookcase we're using as a cupboard and hold up the boxes for his inspection. "What kind?" I ask. I hope it's not stale. Does tea get stale?

He hangs up. "I don't know," he says. "My mother makes it for me."

"Darjeeling?" I say. "That's Indian, right?"

"I prefer this." He points to a different box, which is orange and labeled SPICE. "I like the picture of the tiger," he says.

"You got it," I say, and I'm wondering if this is the way he gets treated at home. Probably so. Mrs. Bose told my mom once that she irons all Ashok's clothes, even his boxers.

"Wasn't she, like, embarrassed?" I asked Mom, "to tell you that, I mean?"

"I think she was bragging," Mom said.

While the tea steeps, I go upstairs and throw on shorts and flip-flops. I start back down, but then retreat again. Even for Ashok, I can be halfway human, right? So in the bathroom I brush my teeth and pull my hair back with an elastic.

"Is the tea ready?" Ashok asks when I get back.

I laugh. "Ashok, you are a hopeless case. Can't you even take a tea bag out of a mug? Watch closely." I remove the tea bag and hand him the mug. "Your tea, sir."

Ashok looks embarrassed, and then I feel bad for teasing him. "It's okay," I say. "You're not a trained professional in the hospitality industry, like I am. Do you want sugar? Or Sweet'N Low? The new studies say it doesn't cause cancer after all."

Ashok says no, but then he takes a sip and makes a face.

"I bet your mom puts something in it, and you don't even know," I say. "What about honey?" I get a jar from the bookcase, then I pour coffee for myself and sit down on the sofa next to Ashok. He asks me how much honey to put into the tea, and I say try a teaspoon at first. He takes another sip. "Better."

"Want some cereal?" I ask.

Ashok smiles. "Jane the Cereal Queen," he says. "How many varieties do you keep these days?"

Now I'm embarrassed. I wouldn't have expected Ashok to remember how much I love cereal. "Not so many," I say. But when I look over at the shelves, I see Mom must have gone to the store. There is a neat line of cereal boxes where books ought to be. I'm embarrassed again. "I guess there are quite a few."

Ashok laughs. "Your mom should use her librarian's skills to index them, Jane."

"Funny," I say. "What kind do you want?"

Ashok reads the names: "Cheerios, Honey Nut Cheerios, Just Right, Grape-Nuts, Oatmeal Squares, Lucky Charms— Lucky Charms?" Ashok shakes his head. "My mother would never purchase these!"

"They have vitamins," I say. "Read the label. And no hydrogenated oils, either."

"But so much sugar?" Ashok raises his eyebrows.

"Sugar won't hurt you provided you burn off the calories. It comes from plants. Sugarcane, sugar beets, corn. . . ." I shrug. "Fruits and vegetables."

"In that case I had better choose Lucky Charms. I need to keep up my strength," Ashok says.

I pour him a bowl and—because I did not run this morning—choose Grape-Nuts for myself.

"This reminds me of our tea parties," Ashok says after a few minutes. "Do you remember, Jane? When we were children? Only the tea was sand and the cookies were made of mud."

We talk about when we were little. I remind Ashok about dancing to "Barbie Girl," but he pretends he doesn't remember. Really, I think he's just embarrassed about the feather boa.

"Do you remember the Halloween we trick-or-treated?" Ashok asks. "You hit me with your magic wand."

"Never!"

Ashok nods. "You made me cry, Jane. I believe you were an ice fairy, or some other nonsense. My mother was so angry. She said your mother never should have let you carry a weapon."

"Ashok, *now* I remember. You snatched the last Snickers bar—right out of my treat bag, too. You had it coming." I shake my head. "Your mother *always* took your side."

Ashok shakes his head. "I am sure I *never* stole candy, Jane. How can you say such a thing?" His tone is serious, but his eyes are laughing. He remembers. "And besides," he says, "what are mothers for if not to take your side?"

I snort. "Not my mother," and my voice is more harsh than I mean it to be.

"What is it, Jane?" Ashok asks. "Does this have something to do with the day you cried in my garage?"

I have absolutely no intention of confiding in the boy genius next door. He might know everything about nuclei and quarks, but he knows zip about girls or romance or divorced

157

parents who don't happen to make tea for you, not to mention iron your underwear. "It's too complicated to explain," I say. "Forget it."

But over the rim of his mug, Ashok gives me this sympathetic look, and I can't help adding, "It's partly my mom's fault I broke up with my boyfriend, with Elliot. Remember when your mom told her what time I got in that night? Well, Mom grounded me—"

"Oh, dear. My mother strikes again," Ashok says.

"Well, kind of," I admit. "But the point is, I couldn't go to his fencing match, and—do you really want to hear all this?"

Ashok nods. And he turns out to be a great listener. Of course, I don't tell him about Stacy's house. I more blame everything on my own mom, which isn't entirely fair, but it does make the story simpler. Ashok smiles at the funny parts, frowns at the sad parts, and looks appropriately mad every time I mention my mother. In the end I even tell him about the "nah-nah-nah-NAH-nah" look when Elliot came out of the walk-in.

"So that is love," Ashok says. "It sounds very hard, Jane."

I am touched, and a little bit flattered. "It feels awful to be rejected, you know?" I say. "But talking to you makes me feel better. Thanks."

Ashok says, "Listening to you is a pleasure, Jane," and his eyes hold mine for a couple of seconds, and I realize I am half thinking that Ashok, the genius, might sometimes think about aspects of the universe beyond math and science. I don't have time to think more about this, though, because Ashok looks at his watch and says, "Oh, my goodness, the time! I have an appointment on campus. I must shower and change. Where are my parents?"

"Don't they leave anything open?" I ask. "The basement? There's no key under the mat or in a flower pot or something?"

"No. We come from Mumbai, Jane—the big city. There are many poor people there, desperate people. My parents lock everything tightly."

I stand up. "Well, then there's only one thing to do."

"What is that?"

"We'll have to break in," I say.

Jane the Burglar.

Chapter Thirty-one

Reason Thirty-one: Because boys make terrible burglars.

Ashok wasn't kidding when he said his family locks up tight. We have walked around the house twice checking every possible way in, and the best we can do is the kitchen window. It is open just a crack.

It's a few minutes before eleven—I still can't believe I'm even awake this early—and already the day is getting sticky. My hair is trying to frizz its way out of the elastic. Sweat beads are forming at the small of my back.

I make my voice confident because Ashok is so worried about doing this, about being late for his appointment, about *everything.* "It will be easy," I say. "My mom used to lock us out all the time, so I know the drill. Do you have a ladder?"

"In the garage. But it's locked, too," Ashok says.

"I could get a stepladder from my house, but the ground is soft in the flower bed here," I say. "The stepladder would probably sink in. Do you think you can boost me up?"

"What if the police drive by? What if they arrest us?" Ashok asks.

"Ashok, would you simply *chill*? If the police drive by, we'll explain the situation. They'll probably help us."

Ashok looks doubtful.

"Look," I say, "you are the one in a hurry. You could shower at my house, but you'd have to put your sweaty clothes back on. What is your appointment, anyway?"

"With Professor LeCert," Ashok said. "It is about my project. He is very formal. Even in summer he wears a tie."

"Then you probably don't want to wear sweaty shorts," I say. "I'll jump for the windowsill. You push me up. Come on."

When I was little, my mom used to lose her keys a lot. She says absentmindedness was a symptom of her postdivorce trauma, and eventually it went away. Anyway, when we got locked out, she would lift me over her shoulders and I would open the bathroom window and climb in. It was so easy then that I figured it would be easy now. But all of a sudden, with Ashok pushing on my butt while I scramble like a rock climber up the outside wall, I realize a couple of important facts:

- I have grown up and out since the last time I climbed through a window;
- Ashok is not my mom.

Of course, at this point it doesn't matter because I am committed. So I am trying to forget that Ashok and I are in . . . uh . . . *intimate* contact, and I concentrate on catching the windowsill and pulling myself up. Concentrating is especially hard anytime Ashok says something because that's when I realize his head is more or less between my thighs. I can feel his breath, which tickles. I try hard not to giggle.

"How are you doing, Jane?" Ashok asks.

"Okay. The screen is coming loose, I think. I'm sorry I'm so heavy."

"Light," he grunts, "as a feather, Jane," which makes me giggle in spite of myself.

Pounding the frame of the screen with my fist, I finally manage to tilt it enough that I can slide my fingers between it and the sill. Then I push left and right, trying to unhook it from the window frame on the inside. My balance is not the best, my butt on Ashok's hands, knees against the wall, tummy on the windowsill.

"Almost got it," I say. "Don't drop me."

I shouldn't have said, "Don't drop me." It is like a curse that guarantees I'll be dropped. Which, five seconds later, I am. Right into the petunias.

The good news is that the screen comes loose and falls, too. It lands on top of me, which is nothing compared to my other troubles. Screens don't weigh much.

I lie in the flower bed for a few seconds, and then I try to take a breath and find that I can't. Scary.

"Oh, Jane, I am so sorry!" Ashok's face has turned white. "I lost my grip! Oh, Jane, breathe, *please* breathe!"

Ashok kneels over me, and I think for a sec that his will be the last face I see on earth. I think of my mother, my father, and grandmother. Then as if my lungs are just remembering how, I gasp and get some air, and after that I notice another good sign: My heart is still beating.

"I'm"—I cough—"okay. Okay, I guess."

"The wind was knocked out of you," Ashok says. "It is all my fault."

I sit up, raise my arms over my head, and shimmy my ribs back and forth, expecting to feel agonizing pains. But there are only little twinges here and there. Nothing fatal.

"I'll be fine," I say after a minute. "Look, we're almost in. Can you hold me for a few more seconds? I shouldn't have eaten that second bowl of cereal. I'm sorry. I'm going to take up marathon running, too. I promise."

"You are beautiful as you are, Jane," Ashok says.

I sit there a second longer than I absolutely have to and look into Ashok's face. Did he really just call me beautiful? I am not sure anyone ever did this before. Not Elliot—he always said "cute." Not Josh Silberman. Not my dad.

Is Ashok kidding?

He has to be kidding.

Anyway, he's only Ashok.

I say, "Yeah, right," and look up at the now-screenless window. "Boost me again, okay? Can you do it?"

"My support will never waver," Ashok says, and now I know he's kidding.

I stand up. I brush most of the dirt off. "Ready?"

With the screen gone, all I have to do is open the window and climb in. I lean forward on my tummy, face against the glass, and push up on the top of the window frame with both palms. The window lurches about six inches, then sticks. I grunt and struggle, but can't get it to move more. Maybe the space is wide enough for me now?

"Grab hold of my right ankle," I say. "I'm going in."

With my weight on my right leg, I bend forward and push my head through the window, which is located directly above the kitchen sink. Ashok is saying something, but in my half-in, half-out condition I can't hear what. In fact, at the moment I'm too annoyed to care. It is not the most comfortable position I'm in, and I don't see how I am going to free myself exactly. I remember the Winnie-the-Pooh story where Pooh's tummy becomes wedged in Rabbit's hole, and he has to diet himself free. Irritably, I kick my right foot; then teetering on the fulcrum of my ribs, I bring that knee up and push it through the window, too.

There is a distressed noise from Ashok. But I am busy with my own problems—three African violets, kitchen curtains, and the faucets. Also, Ashok's parents have left for work without washing the breakfast dishes. Terrific. I will probably impale myself on the bread knife in the sink. Ignoring the danger, I force both shoulders inside. Now I am lying on my tummy, my hands on the counter on either side of the sink, my legs and feet behind me in the outside world.

I try to move one of the violets, but my hand slips and it tilts into the sink, where the pot breaks and soil scatters everywhere.

Oops.

The good news is that now I have more space to maneuver. Inch by inch, I wiggle forward till all I have to do is yank my bottom in and belly flop over the sink and onto the linoleum. I am making the heroic last push and tug when I look up—and into the face of Officer Capparella, who is standing in the Boses' kitchen, scratching his head and looking back at me.

Chapter Thirty-two

Reason Thirty-two: Because the smarter a boy is, the more likely he is to be an idiot.

"Don't let me interrupt," says Officer Capparella. "Jane, isn't it?"

I am so surprised, I don't even think to ask him how he got here. "Oh . . . uh . . . *hi*," I say. "I guess this looks sort of suspicious?"

He nods. "Sort of."

"Since you're there, anyway," I say, "could you give me a hand?"

"And miss the grand finale?" he asks. "You're better than the circus."

I know Capparella is a cop and all, that he carries a gun and handcuffs, that he drives a police car. But at the moment I don't really give a hang. I have been dropped into a bed of petunias. I am teetering on a windowsill. My body hurts. I need help, not jokes.

So I scowl at Officer Capparella.

And he gets the message. "Okay, okay," he says. "That's the problem with kids today. Humorless. Here."

He takes both my hands so I can bring my legs in and kneel on the kitchen counter. From here I step down on my toes on the sink's edge—avoiding the faucets and the spray nozzle—and then still on my toes, I step across the pile of dirty dishes to the counter's ledge. I teeter for a second, thinking of that knife in the sink below me, then I lean forward and jump to the floor.

I am positive, what with my graceful entrance and the dirt from the petunias and the dripping sweat and my frizzing hair, that I look totally, embarrassingly bad, if not exactly like a person who makes a career out of breaking into houses. If I did make a career of it, I would certainly have a better outfit. I would have something sleek and stretchy and high-tech, in one of those fabrics that never gets sweaty.

I take a few moments to compose myself; I brush off some of the dirt; and then I say, "Thank you."

"Jane? *Jane!* Are you all right? Let me in!" Ashok is hollering from outside the window.

"Come around to the side door," I call back.

"Ah, your partner in crime," says Officer Capparella.

"I guess you want me to explain?" I ask.

"Looks to me like breaking and entering," says Officer Capparella.

Uh-oh.

Does he really think we were doing something *criminal*? Would he really arrest us? Should I have told Ashok to run for it?

But then Officer Capparella points to the wreckage of the African violet and says, "You *broke* the flowerpot, there. You *entered* the kitchen."

I breathe again. "A joke, right?"

166

Now Ashok is pounding on the door. Officer Capparella nods. "Let him in," he says.

The door sticks, but I yank, and a moment later Ashok comes through. I look up into his face, intending to tell him about Capparella in the kitchen, but then I get a good look at him. "Your eye!"

A pink-purple bruise extends from Ashok's right cheek-bone to his right eyebrow. It is just beginning to swell. Ashok touches it and makes a face. "Is it bad?"

"What happened?" I ask, and then I remember kicking my right foot away, the noise he made. "Oh, *no*. Did I . . . ?"

Ashok nods. "It is okay, Jane. It feels better now. I'll get some ice. Oh—the police are here! Didn't I tell you we would be in trouble?" He holds out his wrists like Capparella is going to cuff him. "I'll go quietly," he says. "But Jane is innocent."

Officer Capparella's face is chronically sad, like he's always afraid somebody is going to add to his workload. But now he smiles because Ashok seems so serious. "It's no crime to break into your own house, son. We got a call from a neighbor, something suspicious. Had to check it out. You take care of that eye now. I'm going to just fill out my report. More paperwork. I love it."

I make Ashok lie down on the sofa in the living room while I get a pack of blue ice from the freezer and wrap it in a dish towel. I feel terrible that I kicked him. "Now hold this over your eye and don't move," I say. "Do you want me to call Professor Tic-Tac—whatever his name is? I have a feeling you're going to be late."

"Oh, Jane, could you do that for me?" Ashok asks. "I will be forever in your debt."

Ashok is overdoing it a little on the gratitude. "Where's the number?" I ask.

"On the calendar on my mom's desk," he says, "in the office."

The office is on the other side of the kitchen. I find the calendar and the appointment—Friday, 11:45, Professor LeCert, 863-6415. I pick up the phone to dial, then I look back at the calendar, then I set the phone down.

Blackening his eye was not enough. I am going to kill him.

I walk back into the living room. "Ashok?"

"Yes? Did you phone him? Was he in?"

"Ashok, what day is your appointment with Professor LeCert?"

"Today," says Ashok. "Friday."

I wonder whether it's possible to smother somebody with an ice pack. If not, I will use one of the needlepoint pillows on the sofa. I wonder if there is a lot of snot and spit involved when you smother somebody—if it's supermessy. I don't want to stain the pillows. Ashok's mom probably made them in the few spare moments she had between ironing his underwear and fetching his tea.

"Ashok, today is Saturday," I say. "I know this even though I am not a genius like some people. Your appointment was *yesterday*. You already missed it!"

Officer Capparella steps into the living room at this moment. He will never know how lucky that is for him, too, because I bet there is a lot of paperwork associated with first-degree murder.

"Kids?" he says. "You all right? I'm going. How's that eye feel?"

Ashok is too embarrassed to answer.

I say, "Better," and I think, *than he deserves.*

Officer Capparella opens the front door. "Oh—there is just one thing I don't get," he says. "How come you were entering the domicile in such an unorthodox manner? The front door was unlocked."

Ashok sits up. The ice pack falls into his lap. The black eye is swollen shut by now. It probably hurts a lot. I don't care.

"What?" Ashok says. "It was locked. I tried it."

Officer Capparella shakes his head. "Beg to contradict you, son. It was open. How else do you think I got in? Door's a bit sticky in this weather." He shrugs. "It only needed a good, solid push."

Chapter Thirty-three

Reason Thirty-three: Because unlike a screwball comedy, a romance may not have a happy ending.

Something has happened to Witch Lady, a.k.a. Andrea, in the last week—ever since we came up with the Old West theme for the parade. She's a lot more cheerful than she was, but she's tougher, too—tells people right out what she wants, instead of trying to guilt them into stuff. You can see the effect of this in the old barn that afternoon. When Arthur and I walk in, the place is totally a hustle-bustle of activity—peons and volunteers clambering over the float like ants on a cicada carcass.

Seeing this gives me hope. Maybe, just *maybe,* we'll actually get this float built in time. It's too much to expect us to beat Panacho and whatever Hollywood extravaganza they're going to enter, but at least Seymour's Bagels won't miss the Kickoff Parade altogether.

Arthur drove us here. We stopped for strawberry sodas on the way, and I filled him and Grandma in on my morning's activities—breaking into Ashok's and almost getting arrested. They both laughed, which was annoying. Didn't they get that I had wasted an entire morning of my waning teenage years? Not to mention I almost died in the petunias.

But Grandma said Ashok sounded charming—like the hero of a screwball comedy.

And Arthur said, "That would make *you* Katharine Hepburn."

"Which I so totally am not," I said. "And Ashok's no Cary Grant, either."

Now, in the smelly old barn, Loren tells us Andrea has gone to the building supply store, leaving her in charge. Then Loren hands me a can of glue and a small paintbrush and says, "How do you feel about ladders?"

"Okay," I say. But I think of Ashok and add, "As long as they don't collapse under my weight."

Loren looks me up and down in a way that does not improve my self-esteem. Then she turns to Arthur. "How do *you* feel about ladders?"

Arthur's eyes widen and he clears his throat. This means, "Terrified, but it wouldn't be manly of me to admit it."

Loren gets the message. "Looks like I'm keeping my job on the ladder, then. I'm tissuing the letters on the saloon sign. I'm cool with the ladder, but I'm bored with the job."

"Can I do one of the ponies?" I ask.

Loren snorts. "All the girls want to do ponies!"

"Sorry," I say, barely resisting the urge to pronounce it "Sor-*reeee*." Didn't I come up with the idea for the float? Shouldn't that count for something?

"Hey, come on, Lor." Arthur must have read my mind. "Ponies were Jane's idea in the first place."

"Fine." Loren raises a palm in the air. "Help Valerie with that one. . . . Oh." She realizes her mistake. "Guess you wouldn't be wanting to help Valerie. Not after . . . Okay. So. What if—?"

"No, that's okay." I look around and see where Valerie is shaping a piece of felt into a horse's ear. "I don't mind."

Seymour's employs so many peons working so many shifts that it's easy to avoid working with anyone you don't want to work with. Since the walk-in episode, I have only seen Valerie from a safe distance. Now she looks up from the piece of brown felt, sees me walking toward her, and gets a terrified expression on her face.

I kind of enjoy this.

I mean, I know it's childish, but it makes me feel powerful. The truth is that by now I don't exactly blame Valerie for kissing Elliot. I have thought about this a lot, and blaming her would be like blaming Ashok for acing a calculus test. Valerie can't help it that she lies in wait for any guy who comes along. That's just who she is.

If I were aspiring to sainthood, I would say right away, "Don't worry about it," or, more saintly yet, "I forgive you." But sainthood is not on my mind. I agreed to work with Valerie mostly because it will make it easier to schedule my shifts in the future. Also, I am kind of liking the idea of watching her squirm.

But it turns out that watching Valerie squirm isn't so much fun.

"I won't bite," I tell her.

"Oh, I—I didn't . . .," Valerie stammers. "I mean, obviously you wouldn't . . . I—I mean . . ."

Valerie looks so miserable, I practically want to apologize myself, never mind that I haven't done anything to apologize for. Luckily, Valerie, staring at the horse's duct-tape hooves, speaks first: "I am so sorry. I wanted to tell you before, but I was . . . I don't know. Scared, I guess? Of what you'd say? I don't know if you know what happened, but—"

"You don't need to go there," I say. "I know . . . I know what Elliot's like."

Valerie sighs. "Oh, I'm so glad, Jane. It's been gnawing on me, you know? And I was never interested in him. Not like that. Not so much that I'd steal him. It all happened real fast, and—"

"Okay, Valerie. Really okay. New topic?"

Valerie smiles. "New topic. Do you want to make the tail? I was gonna work on eyes next. Are there ponies with blue eyes?"

By the time Stacy and Amy arrive, I am fluffing up the black tail I made from shredded crepe paper. I am so focused on my creation that I say hi to them before I notice the tall boy with the fleshy nose standing behind them.

"I didn't know you could do that." Amy looks at the tail I made. "Did you figure it out yourself? Are there any easy jobs?"

"Loren will find you something," I say. "Oh, but don't ask her if you can work on a pony. She gets all bent if you do."

"You're working on a pony," Stacy points out.

I look up at her. "I'm special," I say. Then I notice the guy behind them has a pained expression on his face. Who is he, anyway?

Stacy says, "So special they assigned you the pony's patoot?"

"It suits my unique talents," I say.

Now Amy points to the pained-looking guy. "This is Doug," she says. "You know him from school, right? Doug, this is Jane. He didn't have anything else to do, so here he is."

Oh my gosh, my friends are fixing me up! I don't know whether to be embarrassed, furious, or grateful, and I feel my face registering all these reactions before I take a breath, smile a lame smile, and nod at poor Doug.

He nods back and says, "Hey."

I don't know what else to say, so I ask him, "How do you feel about ladders?"

He shrugs. "Cool."

"Then Loren will be totally glad to see you," I say. "See her? She's up there, making the *L* in *SALOON*."

Stacy and Doug turn to walk toward Loren. Amy stays back long enough to whisper in exasperation: "Very friendly. 'How do you feel about ladders?'"

I want to protest that Doug is their idea, not mine, but Amy scoots off, leaving me to study Doug Blanders's renowned butt as it makes its way across the barn. Doug's is the sturdy, square kind of boy butt. It isn't bad. Unfortunately, Elliot's more elongated, hollowed-out style is better—or at least, more to my taste—and I can't help but compare the two. I guess I'm staring, because a minute later I realize Valerie is next to me, staring, too, and she says, "How come no one introduced *me*?"

* * *

174

Seymour sends over pizza and sodas for dinner. We are all *really* glad he didn't send bagels. The break lasts only half an hour, but it gives us time to see what's been done so far. The front of the saloon is done but for the letter *N* on the sign. Two of the ponies are finished, but the third one can't be tissued till it gets surgery to repair the chicken wire in the forelegs. It keeps collapsing, so right now the poor thing seems to be praying. The town is supposed to have a backdrop of mountains, clouds, and sky. The canvas for this has been nailed in place and some of the scenery sketched in with oil pencils, but the painting hasn't started yet.

All in all, though, Witch Lady—back from her run to the building supply store—is satisfied with how it's going, and that's what she says.

"A few more things," she adds, "and then I'm going and leaving Matt with the keys to lock up. Can anybody pick up some water bazookas for Seymour and Mr. Black to use in the parade? I want to get all the props assembled this week so we still have time to troubleshoot."

Stacy surprises me by volunteering. I figure she's more into this than I thought, but then she leans over and says she's watching her sister's kids on Monday—she might as well take them to the toy store at the mall. Do I want to go? Does Amy?

Amy thinks she can squeeze a mall run in after her judo class. I'm not working till afternoon.

Witch Lady is still talking. "Now don't anybody stay too late. We're on schedule, even ahead. Oh—and thanks, everybody. Thanks a lot. You've really worked hard."

I think Witch Lady actually cracks a smile when she says

"worked hard," but when I ask Stacy, she says my eyes must be failing me.

During dinner Doug sits on a hay bale with Stacy, Amy, and me. After a few minutes Valerie comes over and sits with us, and—what else can I do?—I introduce her to Doug. He has a big bite of pizza in his mouth, the cheese gluing his teeth together, making it hard for him to speak. In fact, he seems in general to be a man of few words but a hearty appetite for pizza. When he does come up for air, though, I notice that his shy smile is even nicer than his butt.

As for that nose—I wish Stacy hadn't described it as raw biscuit dough. That's a little too close to the truth, and more than once I find myself wanting to laugh when I look at Doug's face.

But looks are superficial, right? What counts is the soul or the mind or the heart—whatever you want to call it. And surely that nice smile says more about his soul than his nose does.

Could I actually imagine *liking* this guy?

Could I ever again like *any* guy?

With Elliot the attraction was overwhelming and immediate—ions to a magnet. Of course, the attraction was also poison, which just goes to show that the universe is unfair—not exactly news.

After the pizza boxes are cleared away and the cans and bottles tossed into recycling bins, we go back to work. Doug climbs the ladder to complete the SALOON sign, and with pliers Arthur performs the needed surgery on the forelegs of the pony. Tiffany and a friend of hers from church start painting the purple mountains, leaving the snowcapped peaks white.

For a while, in other words, everybody is terribly busy and working terribly hard at just exactly what they are supposed to be doing. But this doesn't last.

Chapter Thirty-four

Reason Thirty-four: Because there will always be girls like Valerie.

At a few minutes past eight, Rushad, who has been working for Seymour's on and off for two years and has endured an unexplainable crush on Liz for almost that long, sticks his foot out in front of her as she walks by him carrying cans of paint. This is a bad way for Rushad to show his crush, but I happen to know he sneaked an airline bottle of rum into the barn and poured it into the Coke he drank with his pizza. I guess the rum has made him brave and stupid.

Liz never pays attention to where she's going, anyway, plus she's never all that steady on her feet. She doesn't see Rushad's foot, trips over it, and falls forward, sloshing white paint as she goes.

Once on the ground, she shrieks and calls Rushad every bad name I ever heard—whether from TV, or the elementary school playground, or Shakespeare class.

Not that many people saw Rushad stick out his foot, but everybody sees Liz's reaction. Rushad turns red as a raspberry. "I am so sorry; I didn't mean to," he says. Then he offers his hand to help Liz up.

If you ask me, Rushad should have to suffer for tripping a person carrying heavy cans of paint—not to mention for that lame "I didn't mean to" excuse—but instead what happens is that Liz takes his hand, pulls herself up, and kisses him on the cheek!

Is it possible all this time she has had a crush on him, too?

Now everybody is laughing and applauding, and a second later Matt, who has been helping Amy to bolt the poker table to the deck of the float, gives her this big bear hug, and Amy hugs back. Did she forget about her bassoon player?

It's not long before many other surprised and surprising interactions take place, and soon there is a lot more smooching than float building going on. Established couples are seeking out dark corners, while spontaneous couples are giggling and holding hands on hay bales.

Of course, not everybody joins in. Stacy, for example, is between honeys and available, but she finds herself beside Arthur. Is Arthur gay? I don't know. I have never come right out and asked. But he'd never be interested in Stacy.

So the two of them sweep up tissue, staples, and sawdust while laughing and making catty remarks about everybody else.

Tiffany sees the way Mary is looking at Dean-o, a friend of Shuja's from soccer, and announces that she and Mary are leaving because she has to get up early for church. Mary goes along, but Dean-o slips her a piece of red tissue. I bet it has his screen name written on it.

And what about me?

I laugh along with everybody else at Rushad and Liz. Then I look up and see none other than Doug Blanders beside me.

Well, why not?

But how do I do this, anyway? Do I bump into his elbow? Punch him in the ribs?

Doug looks down and smiles his nice smile, and I see that his brown eyes are nice, too. Maybe this won't be so hard. I mean, I barely notice the nose.

He says, "What was that girl's name again?"

"Girl? What girl?"

"The one, you know, who made the pony's head? The one who ate with us?"

I can't believe it. *"Valerie?"*

"Yeah, that's it." He looks around. "Where'd she go?"

It is almost nine o'clock when Mr. Black arrives.

"Hello? People?" he hollers. "Am I in the right place?"

At the sound of his voice, kids jump apart, blush, and tug at their clothing like somebody's parents just walked in. Luckily, this particular parent has bad eyesight and, it looks like, a lot on his mind.

"Is Andrea here?" Mr. Black asks me.

Of course, I am doing nothing more sinful than tapping paint cans closed with a hammer, but even so, I'm startled to see him. *"Mr. Black!"* I squeal. "No—no, she went home. Uh . . . did you come to work on the float? We're just cleaning up."

"What do I know about working on a float? If Andrea's not here, who's in charge?" By now Mr. Black's eyes have adjusted, and he is looking around, suspicious.

"Matt's got the keys," I say.

"Where is he?" Mr. Black asks. "I'll only talk to the man in charge." Mr. Black is acting weird—even for Mr. Black. I'm relieved when I spot Matt coming toward us. "I'm here," he says. "What's up?"

Matt's face, I notice, is shiny and pink with Amy's lip gloss.

"They tried to hire me for espionage!" Mr. Black says.

The thought of Mr. Black together with espionage is so ridiculous, I have to bite my lip.

Matt asks, "Who tried to hire you? Spy on what?"

"Strawberry cream cheese." Mr. Black shakes his head. "*That's* what they offered to pay me. *Feh!* They did not know to whom they spoke. I *abhor* strawberry cream cheese! I told them no way, not even for *lox* would I do it. But then I worried—should I have said yes? Become a double agent per-haps? I've seen every double-O seven movie, every Hitchcock. I know what's what."

Matt looks at me. "Uh-huh," he says. "Maybe you'd like to talk to Witch La—I mean, Andrea, in the morning?"

"It can't wait till morning! By then they may have employed someone else! By then they may know *all*!"

"Know all *what*?" I say.

"About our float! *High Noon!* The Old West!"

Light is dawning. "They tried to hire you to spy on the build? To tell them about the float?" Matt asks.

Mr. Black is getting exasperated. "That's what I'm saying, isn't it? Don't they teach the English language in our schools anymore?" He looks around again. "Or are they too busy teaching you kids about sex?"

"But who is *they*?" I ask. "You mean Panacho's? You mean Stan Zilchberg?"

Mr. Black throws up his hands. *"What else have I been saying?"*

Chapter Thirty-five

Reason Thirty-five: Because boys are self-absorbed.

(In the dim light of Arthur's ancient Mustang, on our way home from the barn, Arthur in the driver's seat and me, Jane, beside him. From deserted country roads to the big city lights of College Springs. Occasionally Arthur must shift gears.)

ARTHUR: Stan Zilchberg offered Mr. Black a lifetime supply of strawberry cream cheese if Mr. Black would tell him details about this year's Seymour's float. That cannot possibly be right, Jane. Please tell me I'm confused.

ME: I'm not sure it was a *lifetime* supply. It might only have been a whole *lot* of strawberry cream cheese. Panacho had that promotion going, remember? Maybe they had extra.

ARTHUR: They must be crazy over there at Panacho. Who would pay somebody in cream cheese? And Mr. Black would not be *my* first choice for spy.

ME: I thought you guys were getting along great.

ARTHUR: We do, provided we stick to movies as a topic. As soon as we shift to anything else—like politics or fashion—we argue, and then I start worrying about my delicate cranium.

ME: You mean you think he'll hit you in the head again?

ARTHUR: Let's say I'm glad he's put away that picket sign.

ME: And now he seems to be loyal to Seymour's, too.

ARTHUR: What did Matt say to him?

ME: Matt was great. Surprisingly great. It must've been because Amy mushed lip gloss all over his face. He must've been feeling . . . I don't know—

ARTHUR: Powerful.

ME: Yeah. Powerful. Anyway, he acted like he was taking Mr. Black real seriously. He said he would alert Witch Lady right away, and she could pass the word to Seymour and the rest of the peons.

ARTHUR: Matt said "alert"?

ME: That was a good word, wasn't it? It impressed Mr. Black. I could tell. He went home happy—unlike some of us.

ARTHUR: *I* am perfectly happy. I had the best time talking to Stacy. She's hilarious. How come you never told me that?

ME *(thoughtful pause):* I don't think of her as hilarious. I think of her more as supportive. She cares a lot about her friends, takes care of us.

ARTHUR: Yeah? Do her friends need taking care of?

ME: Well, everybody does sometimes.

ARTHUR: Not me. I take care of myself.

ME: What about when you were lying on the sidewalk with a bump on your head? It took Capparella, and the ambulance guys, and me, and Amy, and Dr. Stacy. It was like 'all the king's horses, all the king's men.'

ARTHUR: Are you comparing me to an egg?

ME: Everybody's fragile sometimes, Arthur. You like to pretend you're not, but you are. *(Another pause.)* Arthur?

ARTHUR *(looks over at me, warily):* That's my name.

ME: I'm serious now. When you got hit in the head, I heard Capparella talking to Seymour. He said . . . he said he didn't think your parents would even notice the lump.

ARTHUR: Capparella, the cop? He said that?

ME *(nods seriously)*.

ARTHUR: Well, well, well. I guess he's smarter than I thought.

ME: They really didn't *notice*?

ARTHUR: They don't see me much.

ME: But you live in the same house.

ARTHUR: I keep to myself.

ME *(thoughtful):* I've never even met your parents, never even talked to them.

ARTHUR: I don't need parents. I was born a grown-up.

ME: Come on, Arthur, be serious.

ARTHUR: I am serious.

ME: Your parents are divorced, right? How old were you?

ARTHUR: When they got divorced? Which time?

ME: Which *time*?

ARTHUR: I can hardly keep track. My parents have been married and divorced and remarried a lot.

ME: To each other?

ARTHUR: Not always.

ME: You've never told me this.

ARTHUR: Why would I? Why worry about it? Lots of people's parents are divorced, Jane. Shuja's mom is *dead*. Somehow, we all keep swimming.

ME: Maybe this is why you wear skirts, Arthur. Skirts are like a *symptom* that your parents neglected you.

ARTHUR *(annoyed):* Skirts might be a symptom, Jane, but only of my superior fashion sense.

ME: Now you're mad at me.

ARTHUR: I am not mad at you.

ME: You don't like it that I've figured you out.

ARTHUR *(looks over at me):* All right, then—fair's fair. Let's figure Jane out. Why did you say some of us *aren't* going home happy?

ME: I didn't think you even heard me.

ARTHUR: I heard you. I just got distracted when you mentioned Dr. Stacy. *(Pauses, more kindly.)* Aren't you happy?

ME *(eye roll):* No!

ARTHUR: Why not?

ME *(eye roll):* Earth to Arthur? Weren't you paying any attention?

ARTHUR: To the grope-and-groan at the barn? Sure. The doctor and I saw the whole thing. Some *very* unfortunate hookups, if you ask me.

ME: Exactly!

ARTHUR: And that's what made you unhappy? You're worried about everyone *else*'s happy ending? I never *knew* you to be so selfless.

ME: I am *not* selfless. I am as self-absorbed as you are, and I'm only unhappy because I lost out . . . and to Valerie, too! Valerie strikes again!

ARTHUR *(smiles):* You mean the way old biscuit-nose made a beeline for her as soon as things in the barn heated up? Well, what do you expect, Jane? I might've done the same thing. You're so intimidating!

ME: Me? *What?*

ARTHUR: You don't even know it, do you? The vibes you give off aren't exactly come-and-get-me. More like come-close-and-I'll-bite. A guy like Elliot saw it as a challenge. To him you'd be a conquest—another trophy in the case. But a nice guy, a guy like Doug, he's scared of rejection. He'd rather go for the sure thing.

ME: Arthur, we have known each other how long? Since I went to work at Seymour's?

ARTHUR: And your point is?

ME: And you feel this is the moment to present me with this stunning insight into my personality?

ARTHUR: Not all wisdom can be found on cereal boxes, Jane.

The highway becomes Main Street when we get back to College Springs. Seymour's is dark, but Panacho stays open till midnight on Saturday. People with no taste go there for dessert. I peek in and see only a few customers—but one of the few looks familiar.

"Arthur!" I say. "Slow down! Isn't that my mom?"

Arthur hits the brake so hard, I lurch forward. "Where?" he says. "Not at Panacho! What's the matter with her? Who's she with?"

A car behind us honks, and Arthur waves and drives ahead. "I couldn't tell," he says. "Could you?"

"Not with his back to us. But it *was* Mom, right?"

Arthur nods. "You'll have to have a little talk with that girl about her dining preferences."

Chapter Thirty-six

Reason Thirty-six: Because there's a little bit of Debbie in all of us.

Since Mom's out on the town with Question Mark, the house is dark when I let myself in. Dodging a sawhorse, I make my way to the stairs and up to my bedroom. I don't kick any paint cans this time. I don't turn on any lights. I just sit down at the computer to seek solace—as usual—on the Bomb-Sniffing Dogs (BSD) website.

First, I look at the BSD calendar for College Springs dates that might have been added to the fall tour—nothing. Then I look under "Words and Other Art Forms" in case any sample downloads from the band's about-to-be-released CD are available. Nothing there either. So I check the blogs. BSD is from Toronto, and the guys consider it their duty to enlighten their U.S. fans about all things Canadian, from hockey to politics.

Of course, my favorite blog is Scissors's. He writes less about Canada and more about his personal life—his wife, Tawni, and baby daughter, Romana, the books he reads. Once he even wrote about Peanut Butter Flakies, which is what he eats for breakfast.

Today Trey's blog is about hockey. I skim it. Then I open Scissors's and see that he, too, has added a posting:

If we had an FAQ page on the site, and maybe we should, the number one FAQ would be: Where do you get ideas for songs? (Well, in fact that would be the number two Q because the number one is, "If I promised to do anything for you, would you give me Beau's cell phone number?") So this evening Tawni, my wife and reason for living, says, "Siz, why don't you address that one in the blog?" and I says, "Tawni, my love, to hear is to obey."

The fact is, right now Trey and I are working on a song, so the process—we artists like to speak of our process—is fresh in my brainpan.

This song, which is untitled as of now but may in the end be called "Debbie (not her real name)," is about having fans, and it's inspired by one particular fan (you know who you are, don't you, darling?) who has been, shall we say, overly dedicated to BSD. Don't mistake me, though. She's not dangerous, doesn't prowl in the bushes to shoot my photo as I exit the men's, not like that. So you might think, then what's the problem? Don't you guys want your fans to be dedicated?

And the answer to that is, "Of course, but . . ."

Because sometimes when fans are too dedicated, they make me feel bad for them.

Here is the problem: I can fully understand dedicating your life to eliminating nuclear bombs or injecting ozone into the upper atmosphere or taking care of babies.

But if you dedicate your life to BSD, what will result? Well, we in the band will make more money, and Tawni and Baby Romana and I thank you very much for that, but at the end of the day, even a brilliant band like ours is no more than a band.

Children, heed The Rolling Stones: "It's only rock 'n' roll."

Sorry. Got off track there. Tawni says I should be more disciplined in my writing.

So this song is about a fan. We call her Debbie, and Debbie—well, here is a sneak preview (and Trey will probably kill me, so stop reading, Trey—why are you wasting your time on my blog, anyway?):

Debbie digs us, Debbie dances
Debbie goes back to her room
(Where the lights are always dark)
Sheds a tear
Feels no fear
Pain is part of the addiction
Debbie knows my deepest secrets
But I don't know hers
(And you know I don't much care)
Debbie knows my cell phone number
But I don't know hers
(And you know I don't much care)
Debbie knows my mother's address
But I don't know hers
(And you know I don't much care)
Debbie digs us, Debbie dances
Debbie goes back to her room
(Where the lights are always dark)
Sheds a tear
Feels no fear
Pain is part of the addiction

Tawni's reading over my shoulder, and she says those lyrics make me sound like a heartless cad. I have assured her that the heartless-cad parts all came from Trey, and so now she says, "Well, that's to be expected, then."

Got to close for now. Baby Romana has started to fuss, and it's my turn to change her, which might be more than even Debbie (not her real name) cares to know about the homelife of the famous rock 'n' roller. So I'll just do a sum-up, and that's to say that we get our ideas for our songs from lots of places, sometimes even from our fans, and we do appreciate you, but here's a public service reminder from your old pal, Scissors: If you don't have a life, get one, and if you do have a life, keep tight hold.

I swivel away from the monitor, shut down the computer, get up, and open the bureau drawer where I keep the T-shirts I wear to bed. I pull out the one that says MAN U—the Manchester United soccer team. Amy brought it to me from her trip to England the summer when we all were goofy over David Beckham. Pulling the T-shirt over my head, I think about what just happened in Andrea's mom's barn, about Arthur's so-called insight into my personality, about Scissors's blog.

The thoughts churn together.

I mean, I know I'm not the empty and pathetic BSD fan that "Debbie" is—even if I have been sitting in the dark—but I get this scary feeling maybe I am empty and pathetic, anyway.

My head pops through the neck of the T-shirt.

Am I acting like a fan with Doug Blanders? Was I acting like one with Elliot?

I go in the bathroom and brush my teeth. I splash cold water on my face. I dry it. I wonder what time Mom will be home. I hope she wasn't drinking coffee at Panacho. Sometimes she forgets to have decaf, and then she can't sleep, and she's a total grouch the next day. Who was that guy, anyway? If the car behind us hadn't honked, I would have gotten a better look.

Back in my bedroom, I switch off the desk lamp and drop into bed. When my eyes adjust, I stare at the lopsided sunshine Dad painted so long ago and think.

Doug had helped Valerie carry a trash bag out to the Dumpster. Later I saw them pawing each other in the shadows of the barn. I confess—it made me miss Elliot, or anyway, the physical junk that goes with having a boyfriend.

Of course, it was the physical junk that got me into trouble.

I shake the picture of Doug and Valerie out of my head. I give myself a little lecture:

Q: Is Doug Blanders lying in his bed thinking about me?
A: He is not.
Q: Is Elliot?
A: He is not.
Q: And is David Beckham wearing a T-shirt with *my* number on it?

I rewrite the line from Scissors's new lyric: "And you know *they* don't much care," then I close my eyes, and my thoughts float along with my mood. Scissors's new song is good. I should write a song. Dad used to write songs. Is that why I never did it before? Because I didn't want to be like my dad? If I did write a song, it would be about boys, what slimeballs they are. Or it would be about slicing bagels for sandwiches. Or drinking sodas with your grandma. I will write a song about myself, how I single-handedly cleaned up a small western town while everyone else made out in the dark, smelly corners of an old barn.

Chapter Thirty-seven

Reason Thirty-seven: Because there is no such thing as a hero on a white horse.

The next morning Mom and I eat breakfast together in the living room. I have poured myself one-half cup each of three different cereals; their boxes form a barricade on the card table between us. I reread the boxes thinking of what Arthur said last night—that not all wisdom can be found there.

But what does Arthur know? Clearly, his study of cereal boxes has been inadequate. Take these three. On one is an exercise program guaranteed to firm and tone my abs in only fourteen days—provided I also eat enough cereal. On the second is a connect-the-dots picture that I inked yesterday morning—a dinosaur eating a dinosaur-size bowl of cereal. The third box holds an inspirational lesson from the Apache people, who, amazingly, once ate grains a lot like the ones in this very cereal, grains which modern medical science have now confirmed are totally heart-healthy.

Health, art, history, nutrition. Isn't that plenty of wisdom to absorb along with my fiber and vitamin fortification so early in the morning? If I keep eating cereal, I am pretty sure I can skip college altogether.

I look over the barricade at my mom. She is wearing a bathrobe so old, it has stains on the shoulders from where I used to spit up on it. The cuffs and hem are frayed. The fabric belt is in tatters. The color originally was blue but is now more like dishwater gray.

"Time for a new bathrobe, Mom?" I say.

She laughs. She seems to be in a very good mood. "I can't afford one till the remodel is paid off. I bet John's wife has a new bathrobe—the kids, too. Anyway, nobody sees it but you and me."

"What time did you get home last night, anyway?" I ask her.

"Oh, I don't know exactly," she says. "Late."

"I *know* that," I say. "But what time?"

"Uh . . . why do you want to know?" she says.

I wasn't really asking for any particular reason, but now she's made me curious. Also, I'm kind of enjoying the role reversal. "If it was too late, can I ground you? What's *your* curfew, anyway?"

"You're funny, Jane. But I don't think that's how it works."

"It should be, though. I mean—don't you think I worry, too?"

Mom frowns. "Oh, sweetie. I'm sorry. *Did* you worry?"

"Well, no," I say reluctantly. "But I might have. So, what time?"

"*Late,*" she says, "and that's *all* I'm saying about it."

There is no point making my mom mad. So I change tactics. "Was that you at Panacho?"

She looks startled. "How did you know I went to Panacho?"

"So it *was* you!" I explain how Arthur and I saw her in the window. "Who were you with, anyway? Somebody from the conference?"

Mom gets up, goes to the bookcase where the coffee-pot is, pours herself another mug. Is she stalling? Why? Behind the bookcase the wall is two-toned, aqua and peach. She and John have been trying to figure out what color to paint it.

All of a sudden, a terrible thought hits me.

Mom really likes John. He makes her laugh. Is that who she was out with last night? He's married! He has four kids!

Frank was married, too—Frank, Grandma's lover . . . my mom's father.

I guess the idea shows up on my face because when Mom sits down and looks at me, her expression turns anxious. "What's wrong, sweetie? You've gone pale!"

I come right out and ask her. "Was that John at Panacho last night? Is that why you won't tell me?"

She looks confused, and I almost think that's like admit-ting it. But then she shakes her head. "Whatever gave you that idea? John's great, but not to go out with! I knew I should have told you sooner."

This is exasperating. *"Told me what?"*

"Jane, I was out with Brendan last night. You know—Dr. Bond. We've been kind of seeing each other for . . . a while now . . . in fact, since that night in March when you went out with Elliot for the first time. He came over for tea that night. I remember because I thought it was a funny coincidence—both of us having dates."

I can feel the color returning to my face. Not that I'm necessarily so crazy about Dr. Bond. He looks like an anchorman—all this silver hair, and his posture is too good to be true. Still, he's not married, and I guess he's smart. I wonder what Stacy and Amy will say when I tell them my mom's going out with the president of the university. Will they be impressed?

I remove the cereal boxes from the table and put them back on the bookshelf.

"Well, say *something*," Mom says when I sit down.

"I don't know what to say. Uh . . . is he nice? Does he treat you well?"

Mom laughs. "Well, he presented me with a very large tub of strawberry cream cheese from Panacho."

"That doesn't count, Mom. I think Panacho is practically giving that stuff away."

"So you want to know how he is *apart* from cream cheese?" she asks. "Yes, he's very nice, and yes, he treats me well."

"He doesn't act 'rather superior'?" I say.

" 'Rather superior?' Where did you get a phrase like that? Oh—don't tell me. Your grandma, right?"

I nod.

She laughs again. I haven't seen her this happy since . . . well, maybe ever. "Is that what your grandmother said she disliked about Elliot?"

I nod again.

"I agreed with her on that one. At the same time, though, I could see the attraction."

"What do you mean?" I ask.

"It's hard to explain, Jane. But I'll try. I think every woman—even the most feminist—really wants to be swept up and carried away by a guy on a white horse, a hero, someone to solve all her problems and take care of her and make her happy."

I am stunned. Is this my mom talking? "Did you think Dad would do that?" I ask.

"Sounds crazy, doesn't it?" she says. "But yes, in a way I guess I did. It was that rock-star syndrome—he was up on the stage, so he was a star, imbued with superpowers. You wouldn't know it to look at him now. . . ."

"Mom! Don't be mean!"

"Sorry," she says. "Sometimes I can't help it even still. It's very disappointing when a dream doesn't come true. It takes a long time to get over it. Maybe you never do. I'm not sure my mother ever got over my father."

Like I told you, Mom has practically never said anything about her father before. I'm almost afraid to ask—like I'll spook her. But there's a lot I want to know. "What was it like—growing up without a dad? I mean, I'm used to having a dad far away, but you didn't have a dad at all."

Mom looks at me very directly for a moment. I'm afraid she's going to cry, but then she doesn't. "I didn't know any different," she says. "And I was lucky I guess that kids didn't tease me much. I think their parents were so afraid of your grandmother, they wouldn't allow it. Still, I'm sure it affected me. Your dad was my first real boyfriend. Maybe I wouldn't have been so eager to leap into his arms if I'd had a dad who paid attention to me?" She smiles and runs her fingers through her hair. "That sounds like pop psychology, sweetie—a little too simple. I don't know if it's true or not."

"But didn't Grandma lecture you the way you lecture me?" I ask. "How you have to be self-reliant and all?"

"Oh, my goodness, did she!" Mom says. "Come to think of it, maybe *that's* why I glommed onto your dad. It was my youthful rebellion."

"Do you think Elliot was my youthful rebellion?" I say.

She shakes her head. "No. I think you are much more sensible than I was, Jane. I think you know that there's no such thing as a hero on a white horse. No one can make you happy but you."

"So what about Brendan Bond?" I say. "Does he act 'rather superior'?"

She smiles. "I guess acting superior kind of goes with his job. Should I drop him like a hot potato?"

"Just be careful," I say. "You want to be independent and self-reliant. You don't want to rely too much on one person. You want to see a *variety*—"

"All right! All *right!*" She is laughing again. "Sheesh, maybe I am as bad as my mother was. But anyway, you seem to have absorbed the message, Jane. It wasn't wasted breath."

"I don't know if I've absorbed it," I say. "But for sure, I've memorized it."

Chapter Thirty-eight

Reason Thirty-eight: Because when it comes right down to it, girls are mostly wimps.

I pretty much spend Sunday on the phone. I have to tell Amy and Stacy about Mom and Brendan Bond. We have to dissect Doug Blanders's and Valerie's every move at the old barn. They both apologize like it's their fault I am, apparently, too scary for a normal boy—Jane the Piranha Fish of the Junior Class.

I call Arthur, too, but he says he can't talk. He's putting shoulder pads into the sheriff's costume. It's turned out to be a lot more work than he'd expected.

"Seymour," he explains, "is not a standard size."

I have already told you how pathetic our mall is. Here is something else about it. The only toy store is the discount kind, its walls painted in colors that do not exist in nature. In front of the store, last year's superheroes spill out of bins the size of kindergartners. The aisle shelves are crammed so full that you knock dolls, crayons, and Matchbox vehicles to the floor just passing by.

On Monday we go there with Stacy's nephews to get the water bazookas for the parade. Stacy's nephews are Brian, age five, and Zach, age three. Their mom is Stacy's oldest sister, Diane. She asks Stacy to baby-sit pretty often, so Amy and I are pretty much used to doing stuff with Brian and Zach, too. Sometimes it's fun—like when we take them to the creek and they get all excited over mud and tadpoles.

But the toy store is not such a good place. They want everything—to play with it, to take it home, or to eat it.

Stacy and Amy chase them around, trying to minimize breakage, while I go pick out the water bazookas. There is a whole section of them on the back wall. I immediately zero in on the largest ones. The plastic is a strange shade of orange that will look weird with the cowboy costumes, but, according to Andrea, traditional squirt guns don't pack either enough ammo or enough firepower for parade use. I am planning to buy two, but now I think a spare might come in handy, and I pull down a third one, too.

I pay at the register, keeping the receipt so Seymour can pay me back. When the boys see the bazookas, of course they want their own, but Stacy satisfies them with red squirt guns, instead.

"Are they allowed to have guns?" I ask. "My mom would never let me."

"They can have them for self-defense only," Stacy says. "Right, guys?"

The guys aren't paying attention. They have taken the guns out of their plastic bags and are happily shooting each other, then shooting us. The lack of actual squirt doesn't seem to bother them.

"Let's get something to eat," Stacy says. "Are you eating today, Amy?"

Amy is eating—but only a salad (no dressing); Stacy has fries; I have a pretzel with honey mustard. The food court isn't crowded, so we give the boys each a stick of blue cotton candy, and they dodge around the tables shooting each other and displaying their blue tongues. Amy tells us about the time her little brother used a water bazooka to shoot a Saint Bernard off its front porch, then Stacy's phone rings.

"Always on call," I say to Amy.

Stacy answers, glances over at Amy and me, then gets up and walks a few steps away.

Amy raises her eyebrows. "What's *that* about?"

"Got me," I say. "More important than Jo Winchell, I guess."

Things get even more mysterious when Stacy comes back and won't tell us who she was talking to. "Doctor-patient confidentiality," she argues. "Haven't you ever heard of that?"

Later I'm in my room when my own cell rings. I pick it up to see who's calling—and get the shock of my life.

Elliot Badgi.

Do I even want to answer?

I close my eyes, take a breath, and . . . "Hello?"

"Junebug?"

"Hi," I say, and I am instantly furious with myself because I don't sound icy enough.

"It's so cool to hear your voice," he says.

"It is?" I say, and now I sound too timid. I pause. "What do you want?"

"*Whoa*," Elliot says. "Way to get to the point! I mean, I know it hasn't been good between us lately, and I guess that's a lot my fault. . . ."

"*Hasn't been good?*" I say, and this time I don't think about how I *ought* to sound. I sound plain angry because that's how I feel. "We're broken *up*, in case you didn't know. And *yeah*, I would say it is your fault. All I wanted was to tell you I was in trouble with my mom, and then I find *you* in the walk-in with—"

"Lady Jane?" Elliot interrupts. "I know I've made mistakes. I see that now, and believe me, I am *so sorry*. That Valerie girl—you know what she's like. But haven't you missed me even a little bit? Come on—the truth. A *little* bit?"

Well, *yeah*, I missed him.

But I'm over him now.

Aren't I?

Only here he is on the phone, and the feelings flood back. The problem is that if you're me, Elliot is a heartthrob, and it's not only his looks, it's his voice. It still causes a full-body reaction, the same way it did the day I met him.

"Can't we maybe get together? I'm not saying *back* together. Not necessarily," Elliot goes on. "Just see each other? Hey, what about Tivoli? Tonight? You're not busy, come on. I know you. You need to let me apologize for real, right? It's only fair."

How many times have I imagined this moment? Elliot recognizes his mistake and comes crying back to me, *sniveling* back to me.

In this scene I fix him with a cool stare and, speaking in an English accent, say: "So sorry, Elliot, but it's a little late for that now, isn't it?"

My back is straight, and I am wearing white gloves and a little hat. Elliot's clothes are torn. He looks down at his shoes. I continue, more kindly: "I am confident that out there somewhere is another girl—a lesser girl—who will think well of you one day. Best of luck, dear, and farewell."

But now the real moment has arrived. Elliot is on the other end of a phone line, and so far as I can tell, he isn't sniveling or staring at his shoes. I am fresh out of white gloves, and every time I try a posh English accent, I sound like Eliza Doolittle. So instead of sending him packing sadder but wiser, what do I do? I say, "What time?"

Chapter Thirty-nine

Reason Thirty-nine: Because a rose may be more than just a rose.

When I tell Mom I'm going to Tivoli, she doesn't ask who with, and I wonder if she knows already, if maybe she overheard me talking to Elliot this afternoon?

I don't tell any of my friends we're going out, either. This means I have to get dressed on my own, dig through my drawers and closet till I find the perfect outfit for dessert with an ex-boyfriend—an outfit that will convince him I am amazingly attractive without implying I would take him back in a zillion years, an outfit that will also accommodate a generous slice of chocolate espresso mousse cake.

This is a lot to expect from a few yards of fabric, so it's no wonder finding something takes almost an entire afternoon. In the end I am wearing a denim skirt with a gray-green spaghetti-strap top that Arthur once told me looked good because it matches my eyes.

Of course, I am convinced that the skirt makes my butt look like an ottoman. And I am afraid the top is too bare—displaying my upper arms, which are too sturdy, and my shoulders, which are too broad. Then there are my always problematic boobs, flattened to near extinction by the bra built into the tank top. Oh, well. Elliot found out all there is to know about my body the first time we went out. It's a little late for optical illusion.

At 7:57 I am at my post in the living room, looking out the window and waiting. Mom is upstairs getting dressed. I think she is going out, too. Standing there, I stress about how I'll react when I actually see Elliot. The voice on the phone was bad enough. What if, confronted with that so attractive body, I throw myself into his arms, or burst into tears, or pee in my pants—or all three?

Then Elliot's mom's car appears at the curb. My heart thumps. I yell "Bye!" to my mom upstairs, and I fly out the door.

He is already coming up the walk—just like the first time we went out. But it's daylight now, easy to see him, easy to avoid smashing into him. He looks, as usual, great. But what's that in his hand? A rose?

This is a total shock. I mean, he didn't even give me a corsage for the prom.

I had planned to be all mature and aloof in my greeting: "Hello, Elliot. It's so nice to see you," or something. But the rose throws me, and I say what's on my mind. "You must have gotten the fencing uniform finally."

He looks confused. "What? Uh . . . no. Why do you say that?"

"The rose," I say. "I mean, it's for me, right? I thought maybe it meant you finally had money to spare."

We're walking to the car now. He laughs, but it sounds hollow. "No, I definitely do not have money to spare. But can't I buy a rose for a cute girl anyway?"

I want to snap, "Well, you never did before," but instead I take the flower and say simply, "Thank you. It's pretty."

In the confines of the car, Elliot leans over and brushes my cheek with his lips. My body reacts ecstatically, and I give it a silent little warning: Cut that out.

Belted and on our way, I think, Okay, this would be a good time to ask some questions—like, Was Arthur right that Elliot saw me as a challenge? Another trophy? Were Stacy and Amy right that he felt rejected after what happened at the party? Did I damage his delicate masculine pride?

But he tells me he's going to challenge Ivan for the number two spot on the fencing squad, and I ask how he did in the last match, and all in all, it's a lot easier to talk about this stuff than about the other stuff. Anyway, we have all evening. And for right now, the conversation thing feels pretty natural. I am breathing normally; my heart has stopped pounding.

Maybe, *maybe*, this will turn out good. Maybe he's truly sorry about Valerie, realizes that was childish. Maybe he really did miss me. Maybe things could be different between us.

It is pretty strange walking into Tivoli again. The same hostess with her curly hair and tight jeans smiles and leads us up the same stairs, and I think the same thought, Is she prettier than me? She pulls out my chair, and we sit down. I study the menu. I order chocolate espresso mousse cake.

It's a déjà vu, only this time there's a pink rose lying on the

206

table next to my fork. And . . . aren't I a different person than I was back in March? Haven't I learned something about myself? About Elliot? About love?

Or maybe I didn't quite get it the first time, and now I have to start over.

I want to tell Elliot what I'm thinking, but before I can form my thoughts into a sentence, he asks me how things are at Seymour's.

"Sometimes I almost miss it there, you know," he says. "How is everybody? Witch Lady?"

"Witch Lady's good," I say. "I mean—*Andrea* is good. I don't even think of her as Witch Lady so much anymore. We get along now."

"You mean since I left, she learned how to smile?"

"Yeah, kind of. She's talented, too."

The desserts come, and after we each take bites, he asks, "Like, talented how?"

"Oh, you know. She designs the floats every year. And her drawings are really beautiful, professional. And then she's been in charge of the build, too. And that's going well. She's got everybody working totally hard. You wouldn't think she could motivate people that way, but she has."

I shut my mouth. I am excited about the float and the parade. I like talking about it. But I don't know how Elliot feels. Seymour fired him. I mean, it was his own dumb fault, but still. I don't want to make Elliot feel bad.

Only he doesn't seem to be feeling bad. He's grinning.

"What about Panacho?" I ask. "How is it there? Do you ever have to wear the dragon suit?"

"Nah—it's too small for me," he says. "That's a lucky thing, too, because it's so hot in the summer. The guys come out of it looking like they've been in a sauna. Mostly they've got me prepping."

"Prepping? But that's miserable!" I say. "I'd rather work out front anytime than do all that chopping."

"Oh, it's not that bad," he says. "And it pays better."

"Are you still saving for a uniform? They must be really expensive."

"There's that," Elliot says, "and I have some . . . debts. No big deal. But hey, it's always good to make money, right?"

"Sure."

"Anyhow, maybe you'd like to come and work for Panacho," Elliot says. "I could put in a good word."

I scrape the frosting off my plate with my fork. "That's okay," I say. "I'm glad for you. But I like working for—"

Elliot interrupts. "So Witch Lady's in charge of the float build? That surprises me, Junebug. I think before, it's always been Seymour who managed that."

I shrug. I feel loyal to Seymour. I don't want to tell Elliot that he's been more or less in a state of depression over Panacho. So I just say, "He's not that up for it this year. He's more working in the background."

"And those drawings?" Elliot says.

"Andrea's? Yeah. I found out she went to art school," I say, "but could we talk about—"

"And it was her idea?" Elliot says. "The theme?"

I feel my skin flush. I am proud of coming up with the

theme. I don't want to brag, but it's been the best thing in a bad summer. "Actually," I say, "the theme was *my* idea."

"No kidding, Junebug? *Your* idea? I didn't know that," Elliot says. "That's a funny coincidence because—" He stops.

"Because why?"

"Oh . . . uh . . . well, my fencing, and all? It kind of inspired—" He stops again. He looks flustered, I think. What gives?

"Yeah? Inspired?"

"Uh . . . never mind," he says. "You know, I always thought you were *way* creative. Like the Easter egg you gave me? Amazing. Really cool. Did I tell you how much I liked that? Anyway, I'm glad Seymour appreciates that about you, too. So how did you come up with the theme?"

I open my mouth to tell him the story, how I was so upset that day, and Seymour called me into his office and gave me pad and paper, and Arthur came in, and . . .

And I close my mouth again. Suddenly, I don't want to tell Elliot that story. He was the reason I was so upset. In a way it feels like it was a lifetime ago. But actually it was more like two weeks. When I remember, the emotions wash over me almost full force—how sad I was, what a jerk *he* was.

I look down at the rose. The petals are curling at the edges.

Elliot says, "What is it, Junebug? You okay?"

I say, "Yeah. Fine," and I take a sip of water.

"So you were saying about the theme? What is the Seymour's theme, anyway? This year?" Elliot asks.

And all of a sudden I get it.

And I think, What an idiot!

And I'm not sure if I mean him or me. I put down my water glass, cock my head, look right into his eyes, and say, "You know I can't tell you that."

"Oh, well, I mean . . . I didn't mean . . . Of course, you don't *have* to tell me, but it was only friendly . . . only curiosity, and . . ."

I feel sucker punched—this lasts about five heartbeats—and then I feel furious. Does Elliot's sliminess know no bounds? I can't believe how close I came to falling for it.

"That's why you called today! That's why you brought me the stupid rose!" I say.

"No! Oh, come on, Junebug. Of *course* not."

I pick up the rose, sniff it for good measure, and then throw it. It hits Elliot's face hard enough that there might have been blood—except I guess the florist pulled out the thorns.

"*Whoa*—okay, I *surrender*! *Yeah*, that's why I brought you a rose. Girls like roses, and you're a girl, right? I thought maybe you'd be more *inclined* . . ."

Elliot keeps talking, trying lamely to justify his odious behavior, oblivious to people at other tables who are staring at us. I want to stand up and stalk out, but throwing the rose is all the drama I can muster—especially with an audience. Sinking into the floor does not seem to be an option. Sitting quietly in my chair dying of embarrassment will have to do.

"Would you just *shut* it?" I hiss finally. "What did Zilchberg offer you, anyway? Strawberry cream cheese?"

Elliot looks puzzled. "What would I do with strawberry cream cheese? Zilchberg offered me a dollar an hour raise and a hundred-dollar bonus. And I have to tell you, Jane, I *need* the money. I got in a little deep with the poker playing. I pretty much wiped out my savings—and then some."

"If you're looking for sympathy," I say, "you're not getting it from me." I stand up. "Take me home."

"Fat chance," Elliot says, also standing.

"What do you mean 'fat chance'?"

"Find your own ride, *Lady* Jane. Oh—and you can pay for the desserts, too. I am flat busted."

Half an hour later I am standing on the sidewalk in front of Tivoli when a silver Mercedes pulls up. Except to think, Nice car, I don't pay any attention. I don't know anybody with a silver Mercedes. Then my mom jumps out of the passenger side.

I am so surprised, I stop crying.

"Mom?" I say.

"Oh, sweetie." She gives me a hug. It's been a long time since she did that. She feels small. "Now hop in back and meet Brendan," she says.

"Oh, no," I say. "You guys were out somewhere?"

"It's fine," she says. "I'm just grateful for cell phones. Anyway, Brendan has kids, too. He understands."

"Sure I do," says Brendan Bond himself. He has come around to our side of the car and is holding the door open for me.

It is strange to see him this close and in the flesh. In this town his face is as familiar as a movie star's, almost as familiar as the football coach's.

I feel so humiliated that without thinking, I cover my hot, tear-streaked face with my hand. I start to say again how sorry I am, but Brendan Bond interrupts.

"Hey, don't worry about it, Jane. The restaurant packed up the food to go, no problem—oh, except the car may smell a little on the ginger-garlic side. We've got plenty. Are you hungry?"

Chapter Forty

Reason Forty: Because in case of emergency, you're better off relying on your own sturdy self.

I spend the next four days trying to think of synonyms for fool. I come up with moron, chump, idiot, lamebrain, sucker, and, of course, loser. I would probably curl up under my covers, close my eyes, and watch synonyms swim in my head—except I have so much work to do. It's the final push to get the float finished, so if I'm not making sandwiches and espresso, I'm at the barn gluing, painting, and stapling.

On Thursday, crisis strikes the build when every store in town runs out of brown tissue paper. Finally, Shuja thinks of using grocery bags. This works great, but it takes hours to collect the bags, tear them into pieces, and crumple them. I don't get to bed till after midnight.

On Friday, Arthur makes an emergency call to Stacy. He needs her to make a run to the crafts store. He is all out of sequins for Seymour's costume.

Sequins?

At last, it's 8:45 Saturday morning, and I am scanning the parking lot of the football stadium for a red Ford F-10 pickup truck named Barbarossa. This can only mean one thing. The morning of the Kickoff Parade is finally here.

Barbarossa belongs to Seymour. Parade step-off is not till ten o'clock, but already the stadium lot is crazy with people and vehicles going every which way. I can't imagine that they ever will be aimed in the same direction, let alone lined up in the right order.

Besides the floats, there are preschool kids on tricycles, horses and horse trailers, fire engines, politicians in convertibles, princesses—dairy and otherwise—wearing strapless pastel gowns, Scouts of both genders, kids carrying band instruments, and one million tiny girls in leotards throwing, dropping, and occasionally even twirling batons. The twirlers and princesses come with their own fussing, hovering attendants—moms, stepmoms, big sisters, aunties, grandmothers.

Like most of the floats, Seymour's is based on a flatbed trailer that will be pulled by a pickup. Seymour loves Barbarossa the way some guys love anything with a motor and wheels. He keeps it covered in a garage. He waxes it once a week. He named it after a Roman hero.

I can't find Barbarossa because my brain feels just about as chaotic as the parking lot. Finally somebody taps me on the shoulder. "Jane?"

"*Seymour!*"

"Howdy," he says. "Like my duds?"

Seymour is a vision in spangled turquoise. On his head is—what else—a white cowboy hat. On his plaid vest is a big gold badge. On his feet are electric blue leather boots. Arthur has outdone himself.

"You don't think it's too much?" Seymour asks.

214

I quote from the employee handbook: "Too much is never enough."

Seymour nods happily. "My sentiments exactly. Come on." He leads me to Barbarossa and the float, which are on the far side of an old hook and ladder truck from the Belletoona volunteer fire company. Like all the floats, Seymour's is covered with a tarp. This protects them, but it's also part of the secrecy tradition. On the stroke of 10:00 A.M., the parade marshal will sound a horn, and all the floats will be revealed at once.

Early as it is, Andrea and Mr. Black are at work in the bed of the pickup. Mr. Black is sitting on a folding chair while Andrea bends over his face, gluing on a bushy black eyebrow.

As the only peon with professional acting experience, Mr. Black was the natural choice to play the villain confronting Seymour's sheriff. It's lucky he and Seymour seem to be getting along lately. During the two-hour parade they are going to duel to the death with water bazookas approximately thirty times, and they have to be very careful to aim high so they miss each other, not to mention any kids who get too close.

"If the spray hits anybody straight on, it'll knock 'em down," Andrea warned them. "And keep it away from the tissue, too. If it gets wet, it turns to goo."

Besides Mr. Black and Seymour riding the float, there will be . . . Tiffany, Loren, Robbie, Matt, and me. The guys are cowboys and card sharks. Loren is a dance-hall girl wearing a lacy red dress with a full skirt, her hair piled up on top of her head. Tiffany and I are, apparently, Old West aunties because

Andrea found us long cotton skirts, button-up blouses, and old-auntie glasses. Our job is (a) not to fall off the float, and (b) to lob bubble gum to the kids.

Andrea, meanwhile, will drive the truck.

There is still plenty of time before step-off, so I watch Andrea and Mr. Black for a while. Then Amy hikes over from the FTMB—Fighting Troubadours Marching Band— carrying her clarinet. Watching her, I wonder what it would be like to have a body so perfect it makes even a polyester band uniform look sexy.

Amy says hi to me, sees Matt, and winks at him. Matt blushes. As far as I know, they haven't seen each other since last week at the float build, but they've been chatting on IM. Is she sending him heart smileys? He'll never know what hit him. And what of Tony, her bassoon player?

I decide to leave the two of them alone and go look for the Panacho float. It turns out to be easy to find—the Panacho dragon is painted on the door of the truck. Behind the, tarp-covered flatbed trailer, talking to his peons, is Stan Zilchberg. Now I'm worried Elliot might be here, so I step away and blend into a crowd of cheerleaders and cheerleader hangers-on.

Even under the tarp the Panacho float is obviously bigger than ours, and it seems to be more elaborate, too—more lumps and protrusions. Nobody's ready to admit it yet, but deep down I think we all know Seymour's Bagels won't be able to compete with Panacho. Business has been down ever since they opened. And I guess I don't expect our little homemade float to beat corporate America and all its resources, either.

But whatever happens, I'll always feel good about the float we built. A lot of people worked hard on it, and we came through. The float is Seymour's best yet. We're going to lose, but at least we'll go down fighting.

I am staring at the Panacho entry, thinking gloomy thoughts for the future of the bagel-loving public, when I see something strange. Is that *Ashok* standing with the Panacho peons?

It can't be. Ashok's mother would never let him get a job in a bagel store—not when he could be picking up summer school credits in Sumerian or working on a third theory of relativity. And besides, he had that project for Professor LeCert this summer.

That project for Professor LeCert. It couldn't have anything to do with the Panacho float, could it? I try to remember what he said about it. Fireproof—was that it?

Anyway, it *is* Ashok, all right. His eye is still puffy, but not quite as colorful as it was last week. And if he isn't working for Panacho, what is he doing here? Doesn't he realize Panacho is the enemy bagel store?

Staring doesn't answer my questions, so when I see Robbie, Loren, and Tiffany coming across the parking lot, each carrying a giant bag of bubble gum, I join them. Back at the Seymour's float Andrea is still fussing with Mr. Black's makeup. He seems to be amazingly patient about it. I guess that's show biz.

At 9:30 I can't imagine the parade will step off anytime before dark. But by 9:45 a miracle has occurred: The parade marshals have imposed order; each entry is aimed and ready.

Seymour's is placed between a troop of Girl Scouts with a pony cart and the Fighting Troubadours Marching Band. Behind the band are the Belletoona volunteers with their antique truck, behind them a gaggle of baton twirlers, then the Panacho float, and so on, and so on, back to the last entry, a den of Cub Scouts carrying the American flag.

At 9:53

- Robbie and Tiffany untie the tarp;
- A Belletoona volunteer helps me fill the backup water bazooka from the tank on his truck;
- Andrea paints the final flecks of stubble on Mr. Black's cheek.

At 9:54

- Andrea drops to her knees and whimpers, "Headache."

This is no small problem. Andrea's headaches are the blinding migraine variety, complete with white dots dancing the hokey pokey before her eyes. Usually a headache forces Andrea to recline in a darkened room. She can't possibly drive a pickup truck towing a float in her condition. Can she?

One of the Belletoona volunteers comes over, sees Andrea's ashen face, and asks us if we're okay. "We got first aid on the truck," he says.

Seymour is kneeling next to the patient, holding her hand, stroking her brow. He turns to the firefighter with a hopeless look. "We'll let you know, thanks."

I watch the firefighter return to his hook and ladder and see at the same time that four people are stationed at the corners of the Panacho float, ready to whisk away the tarp. Naturally, nobody associated with corporate bagels has chosen this exact moment to have a medical emergency.

When the horn bellows, loud as an elephant in the next room, I jump. Meanwhile, with a flourish the Panacho peons lift and remove their tarp.

At first I'm relieved. The theme is medieval, I guess, to go with the dragon. There's a castle background, a drawbridge over a painted moat, a girl in a conical hat with a veil, and a boy with a crown on his head. It looks good, but not that much better than our float, and there's no humor to it, either. The most striking thing is that it's not made of plywood, tissue, and chicken wire like the other floats—like *our* float. It seems to be made of some kind of plastic-looking stuff.

Other than the inconvenient fact that the driver of our float is currently semicomatose, I might even start to feel a little hopeful about our chances.

While I stare at the Panacho float one more person leaps on board, a knight in armor. The armor looks cheesy—like tinfoil—but the sword looks real enough.

Then a gruff and harried parade marshal yells at us, "Hey, Seymour's! Get that tarp off! It's time to move out!"

We all look at each other, and Robbie says, "What now?"

Seymour—for the first time in weeks—takes charge. "Like the man says, get moving. One of you kids will have to put on the white hat and the badge, and play sheriff. Looks like I'll be the guy behind the wheel."

I am shocked. "No way!" I say. "Nothing even makes sense if you're not on the float!"

Seymour's upset, too. "I don't like it either, Jane, but what do you propose? Matt's license is suspended, Arthur doesn't believe in petroleum products, Loren flunked the in-car test. . . ."

"What about you, Mr. Black?" I say.

He shakes his head. "Expired."

Seymour gives me a hard look. "So who the heck is gonna drive if not me?" he asks. *"You?"*

Chapter Forty-one

Reason Forty-one: Because a homicidal fantasy is not a sign of mental stability.

The drum major raises his baton, and the trumpeters raise their trumpets, ready to play the fanfare for the third time. Is it a coincidence that the FTMB is playing the theme from *How the West Was Won*?

Or do you think it has something to do with Seymour's weekly donation of bagels to the FTMB boosters club?

The baton comes down; the horns blare; Seymour fires; Mr. Black fires—then he staggers, gasps, chokes, and dies in a flourish of fish flops, after which Seymour squirts the crowd and makes a big show of blowing nonexistent smoke off the gun barrel.

I smile and shake my head. What a couple of drama kings!

Right about now, I should have been on the float lobbing bubble gum. Instead, I am watching the narrative unfold over and over, frame by frame, in Barbarossa's rearview mirror. When I glance at the speedometer, the needle hovers between two and three miles per hour. How much damage can a girl do traveling three miles per hour?

I flex my fingers on the steering wheel, loosening what up to now has been a death grip. I realize something is lying in my lap, and I look down. It's the spare water bazooka, fully loaded courtesy of the Belletoona volunteers. In the excitement I guess I kept it with me instead of leaving it on the bed of the float.

Shoot. What if Seymour or Mr. Black runs out of ammo?

"Turn key in ignition. Touch gas pedal *very gently*. Don't mow down Girl Scouts." These were Andrea's mumbled words when she slumped into the passenger seat beside me and closed her eyes twenty minutes ago.

Climbing onto the float, Seymour said, "Slow and easy, Jane—if you don't want to knock us over like bowling pins, slow and easy."

So far there has been only one scary moment. Every few minutes something behind us goes *whoosh*. I can't see where the noise comes from, and neither can the pony in front of us pulling the Girl Scouts' cart. The noise doesn't worry me, but it worries the pony. The first time he heard it, he stopped, shook his mane, and performed an irritated little tap dance. The marching Girl Scouts would have rear-ended him, and I would have rear-ended *them*, but at the last second the pony decided the *whoosh* would not harm a pony, and he trotted on.

The next time it happened, the pony only wiggled his ears.

Now we reach the bottom of the hill, where the route turns onto Main Street. Ahead of me, the pony and the Girl Scouts stop. I brake with my toe. I do not crash into anything. I do not knock anybody off the float. This is easier than I expected. Maybe I have finally found my great undiscovered talent—driving at speeds of less than five miles per hour.

From the passanger seat Andrea speaks. "Turn wide," she says. "Otherwise, you'll pin the right-hand spectators against the curb." Then she closes her eyes again.

We round the corner. No spectators are harmed. The crowd on Main Street is bigger and louder than the crowd on campus. The band pipes up. I wave. Actually, this is sort of fun. Now we are approaching the Panacho storefront, where the big day is being celebrated with banners and multicolored balloon pillars out in front. The mysterious whoosh goes *whoosh*. I am used to it by now, but . . . it seems louder than before. And it's not stopping, either. . . .

And it's still not stopping. In fact, it's getting louder. Soon it's earsplitting, a growly, scratchy roar like a lion with laryngitis—only the decibel level is more like a jet engine.

I haven't been part of very many chain-reaction catas-trophes. But I bet most of them start out like this one does— with something that doesn't seem quite right.

The pony stops and tries to look around, but he can't because of his harness. He thrashes his head, like he wants to get free, then he bucks twice and lunges. The cart holds him back, but I can see he's panicking. The Girl Scouts see it, too. They scatter like chicks in the rain.

And then the pony stampedes.

He's coming right at us!

I scream.

Andrea opens her eyes, sees the oncoming pony, sits up straight, and screams, too.

The pony, at the last second, veers to the right and side-swipes our truck. I look around and see him gallop past our float and into the thick of the Fighting Troubadour Marching Band. Like the Girl Scouts, the band members fall all over each other skedaddling out of the way.

Meanwhile, as the pony charges through the band from one direction, something is coming the other way. I can't see it, because of the volunteer firefighters and their truck, so I yank on the parking brake and jump out of Barbarossa, spare water bazooka in hand.

"What is happening back there?" I holler at Arthur, who can see better because he is up on the float.

Arthur cranes his neck. "The tubas are on fire!" he calls down.

The tubas are on fire?

Luckily, there are two things of which the annual Kickoff Parade has no shortage. One is baton twirlers—who are no help at all. The other is fire engines and firefighters. First one, then two, then half a dozen jets of water are over the band and rain down on the brass section and after that, for good measure, the rest of the FTMB, including percussion and flag girls.

All this time I've been hearing the mysterious roar, but now its pitch rises like it's coming toward us. And I have a bad feeling it's moving faster than the three-mph limit, too.

It's only when the Belletoona volunteers scatter out of the way that I see what's causing the noise—it's the Panacho float, coming on fast. The king, the lady-in-waiting, and the knight remain precariously onboard. But what is that big green thing in the middle? It wasn't there before.

Arthur yells down, "Fire-breathing dragon!"

And that's when I put it together. The float was more elaborate than I thought—the sweepstakes winner for sure. The dragon must have emerged from the castle, crossed the moat, and emitted a burst of flame. Maybe the knight had battled the dragon. But something went wrong with the fire machine—that was the roar that didn't stop. The float had caught fire, and maybe the tubas, too.

Tubas cannot actually catch fire, can they?

Now my brain is working as fast as the runaway float. Slower members of the FTMB are still dodging out of the way, trying to clear its zigzagging path. Those poor kids riding on the Panacho float! They can't very well jump off now. They must be scared to death. The fire seems to have been extinguished, but no sooner do I observe this than I hear a *pop*, and the dragon burps a flash of flame.

Put out the fire! I think, and reflexively, I lift the spare bazooka to my shoulder: Ready, aim, *squirt*!

But I miss.

Miss the dragon, anyway.

What I hit straight on is the knight in shining armor, who has been clinging to the dragon's tail. Had he been securely balanced, a bazooka stream at that distance wouldn't have toppled him. But he is not securely balanced. And over he goes.

"Bull's-eye!" shouts Arthur, but I feel terrible.

For about one second.

Because when his helmet clatters to the asphalt, I see what I should have figured out earlier—that all along it's not a knight at all on the Panacho float.

It's Elliot.

This would be the time to be all happy about how at last I've gotten revenge on the slimeball. And also I could be amused at the irony of Elliot as a knight in shining armor.

Except that the runaway float continues to run away, and I expect it to ram the Seymour's float in about seven seconds.

The lady-in-waiting shrieks. So does the king. Elliot lies on his back beneath the dragon's soggy head, oblivious to water dripping onto his face. As I watch, his sword falls to the street and the wheels of the float run over it.

Brakes squeal.

Five seconds . . . four seconds . . .

I don't actually want Elliot *dead*, do I?

Two seconds . . .

The Panacho truck hits the Seymour's float. Everyone screams, including me.

Then we stop screaming. The crash hasn't been a crash at all; the Panacho float braked in time. All it did was tap the Seymour's float, no harm done. For one second all College Springs is silent, then all College Springs breathes a sigh of relief.

Half an hour later, the Girl Scouts have been rounded up and taken for ice cream, the spectators have drifted off, and the pony has been tied to a NO PARKING sign. On a dry patch of sidewalk in front of Seymour's Bagels, Amy and a few other sodden members of the FTMB are improvising their own version of "Don't Rain on My Parade." Their damp polyester uniforms have gone all clingy. They look like drowned rats—except for Amy. She looks sexier than ever.

Among the band members there is a tuba player, and I can see that she is okay, her tuba not even singed. Could it have been the flames reflected in the bells of the tubas that Arthur saw? Or maybe "The tubas are on fire!" was just Arthur taking poetic license.

A few minutes ago Officer Giuseppe "Joe" Capparella, mournful as always, came by and instructed Seymour that the street is now an official accident scene, and both Barbarossa and the float were to remain in place until a duly authorized officer of the constabulary released them.

"You mean until you come back and say we can go?" Seymour asked.

Officer Capparella nodded.

Now with nothing else to do, Loren, Arthur, Matt, Tiffany, and I sit cross-legged among the pinto ponies and, supplied with infinite quantities of bubble gum, blow truly stupendous bubbles. Seymour tries to do the same, but no matter how much gum he crams into his mouth, his bubbles remain pipsqueaks that collapse immediately and glue his lips together. The rest of us try not to laugh.

But then Andrea, headache scared out of her, sits down and gives him a step-by-step lesson in bubble technique. Soon Seymour's bubble output is as plump and pink as everyone else's.

There is something sort of sweet about Andrea and Seymour, I think. How he stroked her forehead when the migraine came on. How she encouraged him when he was so down over Panacho. And now she's teaching him to blow bubbles.

Seymour is around sixty. Andrea is around thirty-something. It's a pretty big age difference. But still . . .

Half an hour later Officer Capparella comes back and says we can go. About the same time, a tow truck arrives to haul the Panacho float away. Elliot is still there, leaning on the dragon and talking to Stan Zilchberg. I am relieved that I did not kill Elliot. I wonder if he knows I'm the one who fired the bazooka at him.

I wonder if it's wicked of me to hope that he does.

The way it turns out, no sweepstakes ribbon for a float, commercial division, is awarded this year. After all, only a few floats even made it to the reviewing stand before the parade disintegrated.

Mona Clinefelter, Kickoff Parade spokesperson, tells the newspaper that the organizing committee members hope the community will do as committee members themselves have done—forget the "wholly unpredictable and capricious calamity" that occurred this year, thank heaven that no one was seriously hurt, and focus on making next year's event the biggest and best ever.

Grandma says she might as well have added: "And please, please, please don't anybody sue us."

Grandma also says she heard privately that the organizing committee members are really ticked off at Stan Zilchberg, and if he weren't the richest man in town, he would be permanently banned from the Kickoff Parade and probably thrown out of the country club as well. But Stan Zilchberg *is* the richest man in town. So the committee members have to satisfy themselves with holding an emergency meeting at which they add a new rule for next year: "Absolutely no incendiary devices of any kind or for any purpose will be allowed on, around, beside, under, above, or in the vicinity of floats, no exceptions."

Meanwhile, Mom says she heard from Mrs. Bose that Ashok didn't realize till the morning of the parade that the fireproof materials he was working on for Professor LeCert were for use on the Panacho float. After all, the project interested Ashok because it was an intellectual puzzle. What did he care about its purpose?

Chapter Forty-two

Reason Forty-two: Because a kiss does not actually make you a princess.

Tuesday, September 5, is the first day of my junior year at College Springs High. When I walk into my homeroom, precalc, there is one person I know seated at a desk in the second row: Mimi Wong.

You remember her, right? Even though my mom does not? It's Mimi who finally got Josh Silberman's Star of David.

I have to say I didn't figure Mimi Wong for precalc. But it has been a summer of surprises.

There are still a few minutes before the bell rings, so I sit down at the next desk and—after "Hi," "Hi," "How was your summer?" "Good, yours?" "Good"—I ask the one thing I really want to know from Mimi Wong: "Did Josh Silberman ever kiss you?"

Mimi looks puzzled.

"He gave you a Star of David necklace. In first grade? I hope this won't hurt your feelings, and I never told you, but he gave it to me before you. I had to give it back, though. My mom wouldn't let me keep it."

Mimi shakes her head.

"You don't remember?" I ask her.

"Yeah, I do, but you confused me for a sec because that's not the way it happened."

"Yeah, it is," I say. "Only I hope your feelings aren't hurt."

Mimi shakes her head again. "No, it's not. You got it partly right. Josh did give you that necklace first, but you didn't *give* it back. He *asked* for it back."

"No, he didn't."

"Yeah, Jane, he did," Mimi says. "He told me. He changed his mind. He said you were too scary."

I can't believe this. Have I really had it wrong all these years? Is it possible I was also the piranha fish of the first-grade class?

I must look upset because Mimi says, "I'm sorry, Jane. I never thought you were scary."

I decide Mimi has to be confused. And anyway, there is no time to discuss it now. The bell is going to ring, and I still need to know. "Did he kiss you?"

Mimi laughs. "Yeah, actually. I remember because it was my very first kiss."

"How was it?" I say. "Was it good, or sloppy, or what?"

"Isn't that kind of personal?"

"First grade," I say.

"Well, okay . . . we were walking home, I guess . . . Yeah, that's right, because he lived near me. And he gave me the necklace, and he said, 'Let's get married,' and I said, I guess, 'Okay,' and then I think he just kind of *grabbed* me. Like my shoulder? And he pressed his lips against my lips, and that was it. Four dry, closed lips pressed together." Mimi shrugs. "It only happened once."

"How did you feel about it?"

"Feel about it?" Mimi gives me a look like maybe I'm crazy. "How do first-graders feel about anything? I mean, I played Beanie Babies with Maya Yoder every day after school, and my favorite food was rice with ketchup."

The bell rings. Mr. Patterson stands up and does the usual first-day-of-school welcome and so on—I don't have to tell you—and yes, there is a homework assignment. After class Mimi ducks out while I'm still zipping my backpack. I think she's avoiding me because my questions are so annoying, but by my locker after school Stacy hands me a folded-up note and says it's from Mimi.

Stacy thinks this is peculiar, I can tell. Mimi Wong? Since when are Jane and Mimi Wong friends? But I don't feel like answering questions. I don't know how to explain why I've been asking about a kiss that happened in first grade.

To keep Stacy from asking about Mimi, I ask her how it went when she baby-sat Zach and Brian with Arthur. Meanwhile, I slip the note into my backpack and sling the backpack over my shoulders. After a backpack-free summer, it feels heavy.

"They loved him," she says. "He showed them how to do the Groucho walk, and he promised next time he'll bring greasepaint and they can have mustaches."

Stacy gives me a ride home most days after school, sometimes Amy, too. But today Jennifer the supermom is picking Amy up for computer tutoring. Stacy and I join the river of kids flowing toward the south exit. "Was Arthur wearing a skirt?" I ask.

"Red tie-dye," Stacy says. "He told me I can borrow it."

"And what did the boys think of *that?* " I ask.

"They laughed at first, but then they got used to it."

I have a brainstorm. "Stacy?"

"Yeah?"

"Was that *Arthur* on the phone when we were at the mall with the boys? When you wouldn't tell Amy and me who made the Dr. Stacy emergency call?"

Stacy turns toward me and, with her back, pushes open the door to the outside world, sunshine and freedom. As we emerge from school she is grinning.

STACY: How did you know?

ME: I don't know. I guess I was thinking about the boys and I, like, flashed on it.

STACY *(nods):* Yeah, it was Arthur. He was having a crisis.

ME: I'll have to give him grief for that. He's always telling me he's so independent, doesn't need anybody for anything. So what was the crisis? Or is that doctor-patient confidential?

STACY *(hesitates, a little sheepishly):* We-e-ell, I *guess* I can tell you. Now.

ME: So tell!

STACY: He wanted to ask somebody out, but he didn't know if she'd say yes.

ME: *She?*

STACY: *Nods.*

ME *(thoughtfully): Interesting.* So did you give him the standard Dr. Stacy prescription? I mean, people ask you that all the time, right?

STACY *(nods):* It's my number one FAQ. But this time was a little trickier because it was Arthur. I mean, some girls wouldn't even realize he's a possibility.

ME: Yeah—like he first might have to say, "By the way, I'm straight—want to go out with me?"

STACY *(laughs):* Yeah, like that.

ME: Hey, so do you think I have doctor potential? I mean, if you ever need a sub, I could do it.

STACY: I'll put you on the call list.

ME: Is that what you told him? Say, "Hey, I'm straight . . ."

STACY: More or less.

(We reach Stacy's car in the parking lot. Stacy unlocks the driver's side door, gets in, leans over, and unlocks the passenger door. I get in.)

ME *(buckling seatbelt):* And did he do it? Who—? *(Looks over at Stacy.)* Are you *blushing?* You *never* blush! *(Pause.) Oh . . . my . . . gosh . . .*

STACY *(nodding).*

ME: It was *you* he wanted to ask out!

STACY *(Turns key in ignition, still nodding.)*

ME: And you said *yes!*

STACY *(Looks over shoulder, backs car out of parking space, still nodding.)*

ME: Oh, Stacy, I can't tell you. I mean, I don't even know why exactly. But that makes me *so* happy.

STACY *(nodding, grinning).* Me too.

When I get home, I sit down on my bed, unfold Mimi's note, and read:

Hey, Jane,

It's good you asked me about Josh Silberman first period because I might've forgotten totally. So anyway, thank you because I believe a person should remember her life, you know? Anyway, you also asked how I felt after he kissed me, and I've been thinking about that, and I think how I felt was proud because I thought it was important to have a boy like you, and kissing you proved it. A girl who got kissed was special—like it made you a princess or something. I'm glad I'm not in first grade anymore, aren't you?

So, see you tomorrow—how did you like Patterson? I hope he's not as hard as people say.

Mimi

Chapter Forty-three

Reason Forty-three: Shoot. I can't think of one.

A lot has been happening.

1. Seymour and Andrea announced they're getting married.
2. Amy broke up with the Yankee-fan bassoon player.
3. Very-Nice Construction finished the remodel on our house.
4. I ran for class treasurer and lost.
5. I got appointed student liaison to the school board. (Already I've turned in a list of suggestions for improving the nutritional value of school-lunch options by adding more cereal choices.)
6. I fell in love with Ashok.

About that last one—I know what you're thinking because, believe me, Stacy and Amy have made every possible objection. I mean, they admit he's not so nerdy-looking as he used to be, but they're worried I'm on the rebound, that he's too smart for me, that he's clueless about girls, and they even—how do you like *this* for politically incorrect?—pointed out that we have "religious and cultural differences."

Arthur, meanwhile, is totally for it. I think he's so blown away by his own being-in-love thing that he thinks everybody everywhere else should be in love, too—even me and Ashok.

You're probably wondering how it all happened.

It started three days after the parade, when the doorbell rang and it was Ashok, and I saw him standing on the step, and I couldn't help remembering the last time he rang the bell, all sweaty from running, needing me to rescue him. And I don't know why, but then I remembered how his breath felt on my legs when he was boosting me up to his kitchen window. And then I got embarrassed.

Because this time he isn't sweaty. He is clean and wearing jeans and a blue chambray shirt. But for the bruise from when I kicked him in the face, he looks good.

Later he tells me he rejected three other shirts before he picked the right one to wear to come over that day.

Isn't that cute?

Oh God, forget I wrote that. I mean, I can pretty much hear the squeak of your eyes rolling. One trouble with love is, it always looks so stupid from the outside.

So I will not bore you with every cherished detail. The point is that Ashok stands on the front step and apologizes for working for the enemy bagel store, and he apologizes for making me break into his house when it was the wrong day and besides, his house was unlocked, and he apologizes for the valve on the fire machine on the Panacho float that stuck open—a valve he had absolutely nothing to do with—and he apologizes for his mother (twice), and before he can apologize for existing, I tell him it's okay because I used to be mad at him, but I'm not anymore.

And I also realize he has grown about two inches since I last took a good look at him. And his shoulders are a lot broader. And his nose has this aristocratic shape. And his lips are sort of full, not to mention they fit so well with his teeth, too. I mean, when you think about it, Ashok's mouth and lips and chin, jawbone, eyebrows, his cheekbones, his warm brown eyes . . . Ashok's whole facial package is pretty nice.

So I am looking at the boy next door, the only boy I ever played tea party with, the genius who is always inventing something in his garage, the perfect SAT score waiting to happen, and I feel my heart rev in a familiar but completely unexpected way.

I mean, could a girl fall for someone as polite as Ashok?

Someone so likely to be nice to her?

And had he meant it that time when he said I was beautiful?

Probably you think I stand there in the doorway gawking while all this bounces around in my head and drool drips off my chin, but you'll remember that I am quite capable of being cool under pressure. I think all this *and* simultaneously carry on a conversation as if nothing unusual is going on.

I say, "Seymour just called to ask me to work extra shifts. I guess they're swamped."

Ashok tells me Mr. Zilchberg has sent the Bose family two dozen Texas hot pepper bagels to thank him for his work on the float. Ashok has brought a bag for me and Mom if we want them.

I point out that these are corporate bagels, not the real thing at all, but then I invite him in and we polish off half a dozen. With ample cream cheese they aren't so bad.

(Did I mention I'm going to start my marathon training next week? It's my Labor Day resolution.)

So that happens on a Wednesday, and on Thursday, Ashok comes over again, and we eat Seymour's pumpernickel bagels with honey cream cheese, and on Friday he meets me at work, and we go to the park and eat day-old cranberry biscotti, also courtesy of Seymour.

It's at the park—on a bench by the weeping willow—that he tries to kiss me, and I remember all that has happened lately, the good junk and the bad junk, and that the bad junk started with kissing. So then I get stressed, and I kind of head-fake him, and he sees he isn't getting a kiss after all, and he looks hurt and confused, which, can you blame him? Deprived of the chance to kiss me—Jane the Suddenly Desirable?

I don't want to mess this up by overexplaining, so I tell him one simple thing. I tell him I am writing *A Thousand Reasons Never to Kiss a Boy*, that it's my life's work, that I can't kiss him because that would make me a hypocrite.

Ashok asks me what some of the reasons are, and I tell him.

"But Jane," he says, "do I have cooties?"

I have to admit he does not.

"And are you a wimp?"

I most certainly am not.

"What about Valerie?" he asks. "Would I be likely to fall for her?"

No way, I say.

Ashok smiles. And I realize it could be good going out with someone who is a genius. And at about the same time, I stop feeling so stressed, too.

Of course, I act cool, like us desirable girls do. But I lean forward, and he leans forward, and you know the rest—except there is a little kid running by on his way to the monkey bars, and in the middle of everything, I hear him say, "Oh, yucky!" And what can we do, we both crack up, which is not romantic, but not romantic is sometimes okay.

I don't want to compare Ashok and Elliot, but at first I can't help it. Ashok is more attentive than greedy, his kisses almost like questions: How is this? Do you like that? Kissing Ashok is like having a sweet conversation about pleasure.

And I learn something: If you have been kissing one person, and then you kiss somebody else, it is strange for a while because the new person's teeth seem to be all in the wrong places.

After a while, though, I stop comparing, stop thinking about anything at all, I just let go and enjoy the warm, sunlit sensations.

Later I ask Ashok if he thinks I'm scary. His hand is on my waist. His nose is almost touching mine. He touches his lips to my cheek before answering. "Not right this instant," he says. "But I used to think so. That was why I did not work up the courage to kiss you sooner, you see."

Oh, great. Ashok, too. "I never meant to be!" I say.

"I know that now, Jane," he says. "When you told me about love that time? I realized you are vulnerable, too. Of course, after that, you did kick me in the eye. . . ."

"I am *so* sorry about—"

"Never mind, Jane. All's well that ends well. And if you don't believe me—you can look it up."

240

Chapter Forty-four

Reason Forty-four: I guess I am going to have to suspend this particular life's work for now. But that doesn't mean I'm quitting! At age sixteen years, eight months, and four days, I don't claim to know everything. But one thing I do know. I haven't thought of every possible reason never to kiss a boy.

It is Sunday, November 4, Seymour and Andrea's wedding day. I am at Grandma's, sitting in her bedroom in front of her old-fashioned dressing table. Bruce is at the hardware store. I didn't know the hardware store was open this early. Grandma is doing my hair for the wedding. I am staring at our reflections in the mirror.

I hate to be fussed over, plus this is taking forever, plus the hair spray smells poisonous. I bet it is seeping down into my hair follicles. I bet it ends up in my brain. I bet it's time to kiss the honor roll good-bye.

At least we get to catch up on gossip. Grandma believes Stacy and Arthur are an unlikely pair.

"Is he . . . how to put it delicately . . . *masculine* enough for her?" Grandma asks.

I wonder since when Grandma cares about being delicate. "Stacy says that's totally *not* a problem," I say. "The first time they went out, he—"

Grandma raises her hand like a crossing guard, *stop*. "I don't need details, honey. I'll just take your word for it."

I tell her Stacy and Arthur are compatible other ways, too, like how they both are so independent because their parents are oblivious, like how they both know exactly what they want to do in life. Also, they can share clothes.

Grandma tugs a strand of my hair around a fake flower. "Isn't he a lot taller?"

"Could you *stop tugging*?" I say. "Their butts are the same size. But actually, when he lent her his white skirt, she spilled blue Gatorade. It was their first fight."

"How sweet," Grandma says. "And I am not tugging— you are wiggling."

I close my eyes and concentrate on being still. "The stain came out in the wash. She's coming with him to the wedding. He's an usher."

"Uh-oh," Grandma says, and I open my eyes, afraid she's done something bad to my hair.

"What?"

"I meant, Uh-oh—Arthur's not going to wear a skirt to the wedding, is he?"

"A green satin dress like mine," I say.

In the mirror Grandma looks horrified.

I laugh. "I'm kidding. He's wearing a tux."

"I always enjoy seeing you kids dressed up," Grandma says. "Your prom dress was pretty, but I don't think you've worn satin since you were a tyke on Easter Sunday."

"Don't remind me," I say. "You know what I remember about dressing up when I was little? How much my ankles itched—those terrible lacy bobby socks! I could write a song about it—'The Dressed-Up, Itchy Ankle Blues.'"

Grandma laughs. "That's sure to go platinum."

You probably remember that when I started writing my thousand reasons, I said maybe that was the project that would give my life meaning and purpose.

I was kind of kidding. But it did seem pretty easy to go from writing reasons to writing song lyrics. I even called one of my songs "A Thousand Reasons Never to Kiss a Boy."

I still don't know what I want to be in life besides special, but writing lyrics is fun, challenging. And Amy's friend Alan, who plays French horn in the FTMB? He has a rock band, too. He says he wants to write music for my songs. He says maybe his band will play them.

Alan's band is called Unfair Universe. I predict they'll be the next Bomb-Sniffing Dogs.

Grandma asks if I'm working on any songs right now.

"I'm always working on songs," I say.

"What's the latest?"

"It's called 'Boyfriend Trouble Is Seldom Fatal.'"

Grandma laughs. "I like it," she says. "Can you sing me a little?"

"There isn't any music yet—just words. Besides, Dad's the only one in the family who can sing."

"Have you told your dad you're following in his footsteps?" Grandma asks.

"Last weekend. He offered to give me guitar lessons."

"You should take him up on it."

"Yeah," I say. "And he's got an extra guitar for me, too. I'm kind of psyched about it."

I ask Grandma if we can take a tiny break. I'm getting a

crick in my neck. She says sure, so I roll my head forward and back the way we do in gym class. I realize my eyes are tearing, which must be the hair spray.

Grandma starts back in on the torture. "If you won't sing it," she says, "*tell* me a little."

I hesitate like I don't want to, but I *do* want to, and finally I give in and I recite:

"All I ever wanted was a man, not a knight
He only had to love me, not win me in a fight
Put his arms around me, kiss me till I'm faint
What I got instead shoulda made me a saint
Boyfriend trouble is seldom fatal
But you might wish to die 'cause it feels so painful
Stitches won't help your heart to mend
Only cure that works is a better boyfriend."

Grandma doesn't say anything for a few seconds, and I start to worry she hates it. If your own grandma hates your songs, you'd pretty much better try another career path. Then she drops the comb, folds her arms across her ribs, and starts laughing.

This is annoying. "It wasn't supposed to be *that* funny!" I say.

She wipes her cheek with the back of her hand. "I'm sorry. It was the part about getting a better boyfriend. Is that what you think your mom has done? Or were you thinking about me and Bruce?"

"I was thinking about *me*," I say. "I mean, at the moment Ashok is driving me crazy because he wants me to start running with him, and who has time? But in general? He's a big improvement over Elliot."

"Running is bad for your joints," Grandma says. "And I guess I was confused because *saint* is my word."

"I don't think you're allowed to claim a whole word," I say.

"You remember." Grandma curls a strand of my hair around her finger. "It was at a soda date in the summer, the one when I told you about Frank. I said after I was done with all that, I was about ready for sainthood."

Now I do remember, and I nod, which is a mistake—*ow.*

"So Frank was the guy who failed to be a knight," Grandma goes on, "and Bruce is the better boyfriend."

This reminds me of talking about poems with my dad. "Interesting analysis, Grandma, but it's totally wrong. I wasn't thinking of you or Mom. I was thinking of Elliot on the float in his knight costume."

"So Brendan's not the better boyfriend, either?"

I think about this. "He might be the knight. All that hair? Not to mention a Mercedes and good posture."

"There's something you need to know about Brendan," Grandma says.

I brace myself for some awful revelation. I mean, I already know he's got two grown children and a shrew of a former wife. Is he also an ex con?

"The posture is because he has a bad back," Grandma says. "If he tried to sweep your mom off her feet—well, he'd probably end up in the ER."

I laugh. Grandma places one last bobby pin. Then she

takes a step back and admires her work. I begin to worry she's not going to tell me whether she likes my song at all, which must mean she doesn't, and therefore, Jane Returns to Pastrami and Pickles for Good.

"Grandma?" I say. "Don't you *like* my song?"

"Of course I do, honey. But I'm not sure a better boyfriend is necessarily the cure that works. What about independence? Self-reliance?"

I should've seen that coming. "Both good things, Grandma," I say, "but they don't fit the rhyme."

Grandma aims the spray can at my head one last time. I take a deep breath and close my eyes. A toxic fog engulfs me. "Grandma—*quit!*"

"It has to hold till you get to the synagogue," she says. "How do you like it?"

I open my eyes then twist around so I can see the back of my head, too. I look pretty. I say, "It's okay."

"*Okay?* I got up at 6:00 A.M. on Sunday for *okay?* I worked these old arthritic fingers to the bone? I spent half an hour looking for the right fake flowers? I—"

"You're right! You're right! It's *good*. Really, Grandma. Beautiful. Thank you."

"You're welcome," she says. "And I think your song is beautiful, too."

The wedding is scheduled for ten, but some of the guests are coming from out of town, and they're late. The delay is lucky because at 9:50 my bra strap breaks, and Mom has to ask five women to empty their purses before she finds a safety pin.

"Hold still," Mom tells me as she weaves the pin into the frayed elastic. "This dress is a nightmare, isn't it? I can't believe Andrea picked it."

I was totally surprised when Andrea asked me to be her one and only bridesmaid. But neither she nor Seymour has close family, and weird as it sounds, they credit my idea for a float theme with kicking off their whirlwind romance.

"It's not to be believed, is it?" Seymour said. "After knowing each other for years, we fall in love in a matter of weeks! Sometimes the world is a wonderful place."

The synagogue has two tiny dressing rooms. Andrea is in one; I am in the other. "I think the dress was on sale," I tell Mom. "I think this shade of green was in last year."

"Traffic-light green was never fashionable," Mom says, "but it was nice of them to pay for the dress."

"And they went all out with the food, too," I say. "Seymour insisted. They're having the good lox, the imported stuff. Mr. Black is so excited—I think he's got doggie bags in every pocket."

"Does Ashok eat lox?"

I close my eyes and count to five. I do not see what is so difficult to understand about being a vegetarian, but Mom is always asking whether Ashok eats this or that. "Lox is fish, Mom," I say. "Fish is not a vegetable."

"So that would be no?" Mom snaps my bra strap.

"Ow!"

"Just testing the safety pin," Mom says. "So what should I prepare when he comes to dinner?"

"Dinner?" I say. "You don't even cook dinner!"

"But now we have a kitchen! We'll invite Ashok and Brendan to inaugurate it."

I feel claustrophobia coming on. "No, Mom. No. I don't think so. It's too weird."

"Now, is that fair?" Mom asks. "You used to accuse me of being anti-male, but now when I like your boyfriend and even have one of my own, according to you, it's *weird*." She looks at her watch. "I'd better go in. Ashok is saving seats for us."

"You're sitting with Ashok?"

"Brendan and I are . . . yes. You got a problem with that?" Mom smiles, touches her lips to my cheek, and leaves to take her seat in the crowd.

Seymour and Andrea have invited half the world. Mr. Black is the best man. John and his wife, Mary, are here— Seymour has hired Very-Nice Construction to remodel his house now that it's going to be a house for two. Dad's here, along with his new girlfriend, Vicky; Amy with Matt; Stacy with Arthur; Valerie with Doug Blanders; Officer Giuseppe "Joe" Capparella; Grandma and Bruce. Even Stan Zilchberg.

Seymour can afford to be gracious to Stan Zilchberg. After the initial excitement about the new store, business at Panacho has fallen off. In fact, in the last month Panacho has cut back its hours and laid off employees, Elliot Badgi among them.

In College Springs it doesn't pay to make an inferior bagel.

I am bored standing in the dressing room by myself. I hope they call me soon. With nothing to do, I double-check my eyelashes and find they are curled within a millimeter of their teensy-tiny lives. I pull out my lipstick, dab a little onto my lips, and remember how when my dad left, it was lipstick I asked him to bring me. And then I think of that day in July when I got the courage finally to ask Dad *why* he left. His answer wasn't very good, but it was something, and I also talked to my grandma about the blur whose name was Frank, and asked my mom about Brendan Bond. And on the first day of school, I even got Mimi Wong to tell me about kissing Josh Silberman.

They all told me something, a story. It wasn't always the story I expected, either.

I feel another identity quake coming on. Is it possible that who you are depends partly on the story you tell about yourself? Like my grandmother. Hers could have been the story of a reject—somebody whose lover left her with a new baby. Ditto my mom—left by my dad for Rita.

But they weren't satisfied with that. So they kept on writing and rewriting, kept on working toward a happy ending.

And my story?

It could be about a reject, too. Or a girl who's too scary for her own good. Or a girl who falls in love with the genius next door.

I have a feeling, though, it's not going to be about any of those things—not entirely. I am still working on it.

At 10:15—finally—I hear a knock on the dressing room door. Arthur opens it, steps back, admires me. I smile.

"They're finally ready," he says. "Hear the music? And when you start blubbering, Jane—don't worry. I've got a new bandanna in my pocket, washed and ready."

The End